Babby

from

Edith and Okley

aug- 18 '27-

THE CROWD OF ANIMALS BELOW CRIED, "TELL US SOMETHING MORE!
TELL US SOMETHING MORE!"

(Page 62)

BILLY WHISKERS
AT HOME

BY

FRANCES TREGO MONTGOMERY

AUTHOR OF "BILLY WHISKERS," "BILLY WHISKERS' KIDS," "BILLY
WHISKERS' ADVENTURES," "BILLY WHISKERS OUT FOR FUN,"
"THE WONDERFUL ELECTRIC ELEPHANT," ETC.

ILLUSTRATED BY

C. W. FRANK
AND
FRANCES BRUNDAGE

THE SAALFIELD PUBLISHING COMPANY

CHICAGO   AKRON, OHIO   NEW YORK

MADE IN U. S. A.

CONTENTS

ILLUSTRATIONS

The crowd of animals below cried, "Tell us something more! Tell us something more!"

Why did the king look so different? This was not the Neptune they had expected to see.

Seeing Mr. Robinson dangling there, Billy gave him a mighty butt that shoved him all the way through.

Billy surprised Augusta by butting her right over his head, and she landed in the trough with a great splash.

"Save me quickly, or it will be too late!" gobbled the turkey.

Mr. Watson's hired man soon had a rope around Billy's neck.

Billy Whiskers at Home

CHAPTER I

THE CHUMS BACK HOME

ONE morning in early spring Mr. Watson rolled up the shade at his bedroom window to see what kind of weather was promised for the day when, glancing over to the lane, whom should he see running down its long stretch but Billy Whiskers, Stubby and Button.

"Am I seeing things or is that really and truly my old Billy Whiskers come back to the farm after being away all these years?" he murmured.

"William, what *are* you talking about?" asked his wife, who was yet in bed.

"Come to the window and see whether or not the goat, dog and cat running along our lane are our old pets Billy, Stubby and Button," he replied. "But of course they must be, for where in the wide world would one ever find three such animals traveling together?"

By this time Mrs. Watson was in her kimono and slippers and at the window. "I don't see him," she said at last.

7

Billy Whiskers at Home

"You don't? Down there where the lane runs into the barn-yard," said her husband.

"Oh, yes, I see him now! And do look at the way all the cows, horses, chickens and even Old Shep and Matilda, our tortoise shell cat, are rushing to meet those three. Talk about animals not having sense and feelings! Why, they are almost eating their old friends alive! The way they are all rubbing noses and fussing over them to show their joy at seeing them once more! I feel like hugging them myself! Where do you suppose they have been all these years?" Mrs. Watson asked.

"I don't know, but I would give a good deal if those three could talk and tell us where they have kept themselves and the experiences they have had for I wager my best hat they have had some very exciting adventures with many hardships thrown in. I must hurry and dress and then go out to see them," said Mr. Watson. "I don't want them to think I am not as glad to see them as my animals are."

"Wait a few minutes and I will go with you," said his wife, bustling about.

When Billy, Stubby and Button saw Mr. and Mrs. Watson coming, they ran to greet them. Billy nearly baaed his head off to show his delight, while Stubby twisted his body into hard knots and wiggled his stub of a tail so fast one could scarcely see it. As for

Billy Whiskers at Home

Button, he rubbed himself against them until he almost wore the skin off his back.

"Well, we are glad to see you back," said Mr. Watson, "and we hope you are going to stay with us and not run off right away. My dear, you take Stubby and Button to the house and give them a big breakfast while I do the same for Billy here at the barn. My sakes alive, whom do we see coming on the run from behind the barn but the whole Billy Whiskers family! The procession is headed by Nannie, Billy's dear little wife. From the surprise so plainly shown in all their faces they could not have known he was going to arrive."

"Look, William, look! From the way they are greeting one another one would think they were humans instead of animals!"

"I tell you what, my dear, you see before you six of the finest full-blooded Angora goats you could find in a lifetime. They are all so big, strong and handsome, and have such silky hair and graceful horns. Billy and Nannie are pure white and perfectly mated. So too are Billy Junior and Daisy, his wife. Billy Junior's coal black hair makes a fine contrast against Daisy's coat. As for the Twins, they are their father and mother over again, Punch being black and Judy white."

"Now Billy is back, we can expect exciting things to happen," remarked Mrs. Watson, "for wherever he is, there is always some-

Billy Whiskers at Home

thing going on. See, William, what is next to welcome them! How those pigeons and doves cluster around them, some even alighting on their backs! As they are the mail carriers for the animals,

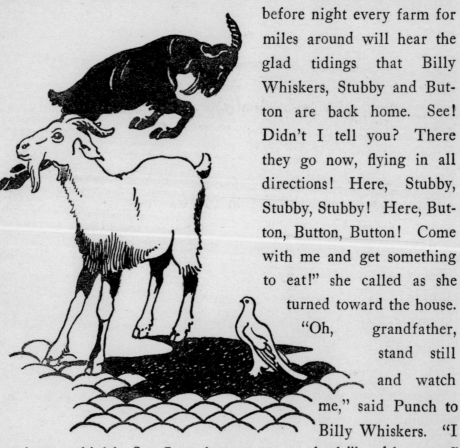

before night every farm for miles around will hear the glad tidings that Billy Whiskers, Stubby and Button are back home. See! Didn't I tell you? There they go now, flying in all directions! Here, Stubby, Stubby, Stubby! Here, Button, Button, Button! Come with me and get something to eat!" she called as she turned toward the house. "Oh, grandfather, stand still and watch me," said Punch to Billy Whiskers. "I can jump so high! See, I can jump over your back!" and he ran off a few yards and then made a flying jump over Billy's back. "I have

Billy Whiskers at Home

learned to do that while you have been away on your travels."

"That was pretty good, but next time raise your feet a little higher for you nearly took a chunk out of my back," warned Billy.

"I can beat Punch jumping," said Judy, "though he says I can't because I am a girl. Watch me and see if I can't!" But just when she jumped, Billy moved away and she leaped high in the air with nothing under her.

"Oh, grandfather, what made you move? Now stand still and I will do it again."

"No, thank you! I'll take your word for it that you can jump higher than your brother; I can't spare any more of my flesh to-day."

"Daddy, you stand still then and let me jump over you," pleaded Judy.

Billy Junior heaved a sigh of resignation and stood still while Judy leaped over him, her feet held so close to her body that there was a full foot between his back and her feet.

"See! Don't I jump higher and better than Punch?" she asked proudly.

"Oh, children," exclaimed Daisy, their mother, "don't always be vying with one another. All you do these days is to argue. Can't you play without quarreling and fussing?"

"We don't fuss or quarrel, mother. We just tell each other what we think and want."

Billy Whiskers at Home

"Well, don't do it so emphatically then," replied their mother.

"Oh, there goes Farmer Jones' flock of goats down the road to the pasture. Can't we go with them? It is such fun to play with them in their pasture."

"Yes, you may go if their man will let you. But I am afraid when he sees you he will drive you back," replied Daisy.

"Well, if he does, we will wait until he gets them in the pasture and goes home. Then we will run down the road and crawl under the fence. There is a big hole we know about that is large enough for us to crawl through, for we were down there yesterday and crawled through and played with them all the afternoon. Come on, Punch, let's go and try it."

And off they scampered, while Billy Whiskers followed Mr. Watson to the barn door where he waited for him to bring out his breakfast. He soon returned with a peck of carrots and some oats, and while Billy ate, the animals and fowls stood around and asked questions as to where he had been, and eagerly listened as he told what he had seen.

When Stubby and Button reached the house with Mrs. Watson they found Bridget waiting at the door—the cook who had been there when they left the old farm.

"Well, well, well!" she exclaimed on seeing the two, "and is it yezselves I see wid me two eyes? And glad I am to see ye! Though I know yer heads must be filled wid devilment ye have picked up while yez were away. And yez had enough to last ye all yer life when yez lift us! Unless time has put some sinse in yer heads, which I hope it has! But here! Yez didn't come home to hear me talk but to git something to eat. Just wait around a minute and I'll give yez the best breakfast yez have had since yez lift, and one that'll make yezselves stick out like barrels!"

"Bridget is the same old girl, isn't she?" said Stubby.

"Yes; her bark is worse than her bite," replied Button. "Yum, yum! I smell something delicious cooking, and here she comes with two plates heaped full of food!"

They had just finished their meal when Bridget came rushing out of the kitchen with the broom held high over her head, exclaiming, "Come along, Stubby and Button, and hilp me drive out that cross old cow that is always coming into our yard and eating up our flowers!"

The cow was standing in the middle of the flower bed making havoc of it, and Bridget charged on her with the broom, but instead of stopping eating, the cow lowered her head and made for Bridget on the run. Bridget turned and fled toward the porch, the cow close at her heels. She was just ready to hook the woman when she her-

Billy Whiskers at Home

self had a surprise for she found herself facing two angry eyes and a pair of horns twice as sharp as her own. And before she could hook whatever this was before her, she felt two sharp horns running

into her side and pushing her sideways. She came to the conclusion that it was about time for her to make a hasty departure. As she turned toward the gate she found herself hurried through it by a little dog barking and snapping at her heels and then hanging to her tail. Though she tried again and again to kick him, she could not

14

Billy Whiskers at Home

succeed, for when she kicked out with one foot, he was always snapping at the other leg.   He chased her down the road for a mile and then with a parting warning not to come into that yard again, he let her go.

For the rest of the day the Chums wandered around the farm to see what improvements had been made and to meet the new animals that had been bought by Mr. Watson while they had been away. And when they went to bed that night, all three declared there was no place in all the whole wide world like the dear old farm.

WHY DID THE KING LOOK SO DIFFERENT? THIS WAS NOT THE NEPTUNE
THEY HAD EXPECTED TO SEE.

(Page 65)

CHAPTER II

SAL SCRUGS MAKES TROUBLE

EARLY the next morning from far and near came pigeons, blackbirds, swallows, robins and every other kind of bird that makes its home in Wisconsin in the summer. They had heard the news that the Chums had returned and now hastened to extend them a welcome on their own account as well as to deliver greetings from the animals on the different farms roundabout who were unable to get away, as most of them were either fenced in their pastures or shut up in their stables.

One homely, raw-boned, cross-eyed cow named Sal Scrugs whom no one liked and at whom every one threw stones because she was always in mischief of some kind, said she was not going to send her message but was going to deliver it in person as these three were the only animals that had ever been nice to her. *They* understood and knew that the reason she behaved so badly was that everyone had always been so mean to her and never given her a kind word because she was so homely. She could not help being homely, and it had only soured her disposition to be treated so and called horrid names

17

Billy Whiskers at Home

when it was no fault of her own. She said, "Very well, if people treat me badly, I will be more tricky and disagreeable than they ever

thought of being." So from calfhood she had *tried* to be mean. She would jump all the fences she could, trample people's gardens

Billy Whiskers at Home

and eat their early vegetables. Then too she would milk herself so when they wanted to milk her she would be dry. Another trick was to break down the fence and let all the other stock out. Consequently when she said she was going to see Billy, all the animals where she lived knew she would do it by jumping the fence in the pasture and running off.

"Listen, friends," she said. "I want to ask you a question. How many of you would like to go to see Billy Whiskers, Stubby and Button if you had the chance?"

"We all would, I know," spoke up an old brindle cow.

"Surely we would!" piped up all the others.

"Very well, then. When I am down in the pasture away from the house where no one can see me, I will break down the fence and you can all get out and run down the road and see the Chums before any one knows you have left the pasture."

"Oh, that will be fine!" said one of the young heifers. "I would just love a lark like that! Anything to cause a little excitement! We lead such a quiet life here with no change from day to day, month in and month out."

"Yes, but how will you like it if, after we are out, Mr. Watson's hired man sics Shep on us and he bites your legs and hangs on your tail? I tell you that dog has sharp teeth and gives a vicious bite for he has snapped at me more than once when I have not walked fast

19

enough to suit him. You must remember I was born on the Watson farm and lived there until I was four years old, when I was sold to Mr. Jones."

"I don't care! I am willing to take the chance and the bite too for a little fun."

"Here comes the hired man to drive us to pasture," said Sal Scrugs.

Very sedately all the cows walked down the road to the pasture and after the man had shut them in, they lingered around the gate until he disappeared from sight over the brow of the hill. Then with a merry Ha! Ha! bellow in her throat, Sal Scrugs said, "Follow me along the fence until we come to the weak place in it. There are two loose posts that with a good hard push will fall right over into the road and then we can all pass through the opening and be free. Free! Oh, it is glorious to feel free!"

Sal was about to throw her weight against the weak section of the fence when one of the cows said:

"Hold on a minute! I think I hear a wagon coming down the road. We must wait until it passes or we will be caught."

So they patiently waited until a big lumbering wagon had passed and disappeared over the hill. Then with a rush Sal ran to the fence and threw herself against it with all her might. Down it went with a crash and over toppled the posts as well. This made a great wide place for them to go through. They were in such a hurry to get out before any more wagons came along to stop them that two or three of the cows fell down in their mad haste to be on the way to see Billy, Stubby and Button. One cow hurt herself badly as she rushed over the fallen rails and she had to walk with a limp all the way to the Watson farm.

Billy and Nannie were on top of the old strawstack, their favorite resting place, for from there they could see all that went on in the barnyard directly under them and for two miles all around them.

Billy had just finished telling Nannie of one of his narrow escapes when, looking down the road, what should he see but all of Farmer Jones' small herd of cattle coming on the run down the road. Indeed, before he could tell Nannie to look, they were turning in at the Watson lane.

"I wonder who is chasing them. It must be some stray dog for their own dog Nig knows cows should never be made to run," said Billy.

"But I see no dog, or man either, Billy," said Nannie. "See, they have spied us up on the stack and are making for it."

By that time the foremost cow had reached the stack and each one was mooing to express the joy it gave her to see Billy back again and finding him as well and as strong as when he had left.

"A speech! A speech!" they called.

Billy Whiskers at Home

Billy stood up on the strawstack where all could see and hear him. "Very dear and old tried-and-true friends, I cannot tell you with

what joy I see you all again, and the welcome home you are giving me touches my heart most deeply."

Just at this point his speech was interrupted by Mr. Watson and

Billy Whiskers at Home

Shep running into the barnyard to drive out the stray cows.

"Well, I declare!" exclaimed Mr. Watson. "Instead of strange cattle these belong to Mr. Jones. They must have broken out of their pasture. Come, Shep, we will drive them back. Not so fierce there, Shep! There is no need to snap at them and hang on their tails, for you see they are going peacefully enough. And you must never snap or bite at an animal when it is going along quietly minding its own business."

"Good-by, Billy! Good-by! Anyway, we saw you before we were driven back, and we are glad we broke down the fence and came."

"Go away from me, you nasty dog! Can't you see I am hurrying as fast as I can with a lame leg?" said the young cow whose aunt had warned her if she ran away a dog might snap at her heels and bite her. "I seem to be the only one that was hurt or at whom the dog really took a nip. But I don't regret coming in the least, for I never saw Billy Whiskers before. I had heard so much about him that I wanted to see for myself if he was as wonderful as all the cows, horses, sheep, pigs and goats said he was. And he certainly is. My, but he looked handsome as he stood up on that strawstack addressing the crowd below, with his long white beard blowing in the wind and the sunshine making his silky white hair glisten like silver! Well, here we are back at our pasture. You may be sure I shall look

23

out as I walk over those old rails this time so that I don't hurt my-self again."

When the cows were all in, Mr. Watson tried to patch up the open-ing but he could not succeed in making the posts stand up, so he said to Shep, "Shep, you stay here and watch the cattle. Don't let them come through the opening. I am going to tell Mr. Jones about his broken fence. Now mind, don't let a single cow out!" and whis-tling, he turned and walked toward the Jones farmhouse.

He was scarcely out of sight when Sal Scrugs said, "Watch me pass that dog! If he tries to stop me, I shall send him a mile down the road and then if he comes at me again I shall hook him up in the air twenty-five feet."

"Now look here, Sal Scrugs, you are courting trouble for your-self! Shep won't hurt you if you behave, but just let any cow try to hook him and he will bite in earnest. What is more, he will bring you back to the herd if it takes him all day. Any animal he starts out to get, he gets if it takes all day to do it," said the old cow that used to live at Mr. Watson's, and therefore knew Shep and his ways well.

"Pooh! I'll see a dog try to stop me! I always out-run them for, as you know, I have extra long legs which help me to jump fences and out-run dogs. And as I always keep in practice, I don't get out of breath like most cows do. Then too my bag is small so it never bothers me by swinging from side to side when I run."

"Just the same you will find Shep is an unusual dog, and he would consider it a disgrace to allow a cow to get away from him after he had been told to watch it."

CHAPTER III

SAL SCRUGS DEFIES SHEP

"ANYHOW I am going to try it," determined Sal. "I can but fail, and it will give the rest of you stay-at-homes something to bet on—whether I win or the dog."

"Well, if you come home with bleeding ankles and half your tail pulled out, don't say no one warned you not to go."

"Look! Shep is half asleep, stretched there in the middle of the broken fence, thinking to himself that none of the cows will even try to pass him! I'll just go pretty near the opening, eating as I go along, until I see him close his eyes. Then I'll take a running jump over the fallen rails and off down the road I'll go. I'll take the road from home as there is a nice thick woods down that way where I can hide until he stops hunting for me," said Sal.

"I tell you you aren't counting on Shep being different from other dogs who have chased you. But you will find there are dogs—and dogs. Shep belongs to the kind that never give up."

"I don't care. Tee hee! Keep your eyes open for I am off!"

Five minutes later there was a sharp bark from Shep and when the cows stopped eating to look up to see what caused it, all they saw

27

was a thick cloud of dust, with Sal Scrugs running like mad and a bundle of yellow hair following in leaps and bounds.

"Oh, dear!" said Sal Scrugs to herself. "That dog is gaining on me! I thought that with my long legs I could out-run any dog, but this one is coming like the wind and is surely gaining on me. My only hope is to jump this barbed wire fence which he can't crawl through, and make for the woods at the other side of the field where he can't see me."

Just as Shep reached her and gave one nip at her heels, taking out a small piece of flesh, Sal jumped the fence. It being higher than she calculated, instead of landing on her feet as usual, she caught her foot on the top wire, which threw her on her nose and she fell, nearly breaking her neck. But in a minute she was up and off again across the field, running faster than ever for now she began to know for a certainty that unless she gained the shelter of the woods and hid in the thick underbrush, she was lost and Shep would bite her unmercifully unless she went back to the herd. And she did not care to return and endure their laughter at her expense after all her vain boasting.

While she was running across the lot for dear life, Shep was barking in anger at the closely woven barbed wires that kept him from the pursuit. He tried jumping the fence, but could not and was about to run around the field when he spied a small hole under the

Billy Whiskers at Home

fence. In a jiffy he was scratching, making the dirt fly out in a shower behind him as he made the hole large enough for him to squeeze under. And just as Sal Scrugs entered the woods and turned her head to see where Shep was, expecting to see him running aimlessly up and down the road, she saw him coming like mad, already half way across the field. With a quick plunge into the deep bushes, she stood still, hoping to hide from him. She scarcely breathed for fear of betraying her presence, but alas, she had forgotten that dogs do not have to trust to their eyes to find things, but that they are given a sense of smell which aids them wonderfully.

The minute Shep entered the woods, he saw some bushes were slightly moving, so he went directly to them and as he approached the scent of a cow grew stronger and stronger. Peering through the bushes, he spied Sal Scrugs standing stock still, staring back at him, her eyes distended with fear. For by this time Sal

Billy Whiskers at Home

Scrugs knew she had found her master and was frightened to death.

"Here you, Sal, come out of those bushes and march straight back to the pasture, or I'll nip your ankles until they bleed!" barked Shep.

"I'll do nothing of the kind, for you don't belong to our farm and consequently it is none of your business what I do!" she answered.

"Oh, yes, it *is* my business because my master told me not to allow a single cow out of the pasture while he was gone. You heard him say it! Still you thought you would go, just to be mean. Now I'll bark three times and on the third bark you chase yourself toward home or I'll show you. And what is more, I'll bite you every time you try to get away from me. Bow, wow, wow!"

By the second "Wow!" Sal Scrugs bounded out of the bushes in the opposite direction from the pasture and hooked her way through the thick bushes straight for a little lake that lay sparkling in the sunshine.

"Here, you long-legged, cross-eyed cow, don't think you are going to lose *me* in these woods! For you are not, even if the thorns and briars do pull the hair off my skin!"

On, on, faster and faster went Sal Scrugs, straight for the lake, though the hide on her back was scratched by the long, cruel thorns on the thorn apple trees under which she ran. Anything was better than being bitten by Shep! She had just come out of the woods to a smooth piece of ground where she expected to make great headway and out-distance Shep when, chancing to look behind her, she saw Shep within thirty feet of her, running with mouth open and showing to advantage his glistening teeth.

"Oh, my! He is going to catch me! But I will try one more way to dodge him. I will run into the lake."

She increased her speed but to no avail. She could hear him coming closer and closer and just as she reached the shore of the lake she felt his warm breath on her legs and expected to feel his sharp teeth sink in her ankles when, with one plunge, she threw herself into the deep water and began to swim for the opposite shore. Shep did likewise, and her hope that he would not follow her into the water was blasted. As she swam, he barked to her: "If you don't turn toward the pasture when we land, I will bite a big piece out of your hind leg, and no fooling about it, either!"

On hearing this, Sal said to herself, "I guess he means it so I might just as well give up now and go back to the pasture as to wait until I am all bitten up. I guess my aunt was right. Shep never gives up chasing an animal until he has it where he wants it."

Consequently when she landed on the opposite shore, she cut sticks for the home pasture as fast as her legs would carry her.

What was Shep's surprise when he returned to find that while he had been gone all the other cows had walked out of the pasture and were now ambling leisurely down the road away from home! But

31

Billy Whiskers at Home

it took only a few minutes for him to run past them and head them toward home again.   He had just succeeded in getting them all back in the pasture and was taking a much needed rest when he saw Mr. Watson, Mr. Jones and their two hired men coming down the road to mend the fence.   When they arrived, Mr. Watson noticed that Shep was wringing wet and he said, "Why, Shep, how in the world did you manage to get so wet?   There is no water nearer than the lake, and I do not think you would leave the cows you were in charge of long enough to go for a swim."   But chancing to look up just then, he saw Sal Scrugs too was wet all

over, and he exclaimed, "I think I begin to see light!   That impish cow of yours, Sal Scrugs, got out of the pasture and went over to

32

the lake, and she and Shep have both been in the water. And I think if the truth were known, it was she who broke down the fence and let out all the other cows."

"I believe so, too," replied Mr. Jones, "and this settles it. I am tired of her tricks and I am going to put her up for sale to-morrow. She never gave much milk, and I can't fatten her for beef; no matter how much I feed her, she never takes on a pound of flesh. So why keep such a mean animal? Sal Scrugs, you hear that? You are to be sold to-morrow!"

"Now don't you wish you had taken your old aunt's good advice and not broken down the fence?" twitted one of the herd.

"No, I don't! I have had some excitement, and I would just as soon be sold as not, for I am tired living my life among such old fogies as you! If I don't like the people to whom he sells me, I shall jump the fence and run away."

"Yes, and if you keep that up much longer, you will find yourself hung up by one leg on a hook in a butcher shop one of these days. But I am only wasting breath talking to you," said Sal's aunt and she turned her back and walked off, shaking her head in dismay at the actions of her wayward niece.

CHAPTER IV

AN INVITATION TO A "WELCOME HOME" PARTY

HILE Billy Whiskers and his family were eating their breakfast the next morning, who should come fluttering down beside them but a beautiful fan-tailed pigeon from Mr. Smith's farm, bearing an urgent invitation to Mr. and Mrs. Billy Whiskers, Mr. and Mrs. Billy Whiskers, Jr., as well as Stubby and Button, to attend that very night, as soon as the moon was up, a "welcome home" party Mr. and Mrs. Spotted Goat were giving in honor of the home-coming of Billy Whiskers and his Chums. The affair was to be held in the hollow between two high hills down in the pasture by the side of the little brook. And all the other animals on the Watson farm were likewise invited, as were those on the Jones farm. Even the pigs had been bidden to the feast of welcome!

"Thank Mr. and Mrs. Spotted Goat for their kind invitation to myself and family. Give them our regards and tell them we all accept, including Stubby and Button, and that I personally consider it a great honor for them to give such a party."

"Oh, grandfather, can't we go too?" asked Punch.

Billy Whiskers at Home

"Do say yes, grandfather!" pleaded Judy. "We want to go so much! We love to play with the little goats and lambs on the Smith farm, and we won't be a bit of bother or get into mischief even once."

"No, truly, we won't!" chimed in Punch.

"I am sorry, but I could not take you out to an evening party. Besides, no children are included; just grown-ups."

"Well, but we won't bother them. We can get some of the little kids and lambs and go away off from the party to play. Oh, do let us go! We never have been to a big party like that," pleaded Judy.

"Children," commanded their mother, "stop teasing. You cannot go and that settles it. Besides, what did I tell you, Judy? If you do not break yourself of this habit of teasing, I will punish you severely. It is a most annoying habit for a kid to have. I simply won't permit you to do it. What is more, you need not go off pouting for that is as bad as teasing."

The Twins walked off behind the barn with gloomy faces, but they had scarcely turned the corner when Judy's face brightened, and she exclaimed, "I tell you what let's do, Punch! Let's run away and go over to Mr. Smith's farm and watch them prepare for the party and play with Mrs. Spots' twins. We can have a fine time before the party begins. Almost as much as if we went to it, for we won't have the grown-ups there to say, 'Don't do that!' to us all the time."

Billy Whiskers at Home

"Oh, Judy, you are a brick for thinking of that plan! It will be lovely. I'll go ask mother if we may go down in the pasture and play in the brook," replied Punch. "If we ask her, they won't be looking for us all the time and discover we are gone. You know our pasture adjoins Mr. Smith's where the party is to be held, and the same brook runs through both. We can walk up the stream and crawl under the wire that stretches across the stream to separate the two pastures. And if we should happen to get on the other side of the wire when wading, no one could blame us for not noticing *that*, could they?"

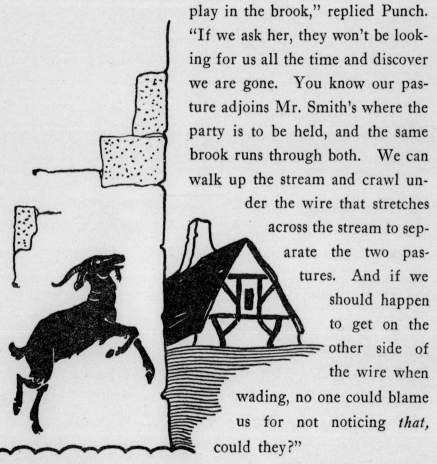

"Of course not! Run along and ask her. I'll wait for you here."

"Mother, where are you?" called Punch.

Billy Whiskers at Home

"Over here by the watering trough," she answered.

"Well, mother, may Judy and I go down in our meadow and play by the brook? It is so nice and cool down there and we love to stand in the water and watch the fish swim around."

"Yes, if you will be careful and stay away from the holes, for you could easily drown in one of them, the water is so deep. But you well know where they are, don't you? Each one has a long stick driven in it, standing well out of the water, with a red flag on it. So you can't help knowing where they are. Good-by, and come home early for luncheon."

"I won't promise about that. We may be having too good a time to come home and we can eat some nice green grass and peppermint down by the stream, which will be a better luncheon than you will have. So don't look for us, mother."

"Very well! Be good children, and be careful about the deep holes."

"All right. We won't go near the holes. Good-by!" and Punch was off with a skip and a jump around the barn.

"Hurrah! Hurrah! We may go, Judy! Come along! I'll race you down the hill."

"It is very nice of Mr. and Mrs. Spots to give a party for us and such a big one, too, for there are dozens of animals on the farms round about us, and they have invited them from every farm that adjoins theirs," said Billy.

"Yes, but you must remember, my dear, that not one-third of them will be able to come, as they cannot get out of their stables and pastures on account of the high fences and the locked doors of the stables."

"Yes, I know that. But isn't it a shame they cannot get away, for they all have such quiet lives that it would do them good to have a little excitement now and then."

"Here come some of the sheep and goats to ask you not what they shall wear, having only one dress to their names, but how in the world they are to get the dirt off their wool and hair."

"Good-morning, Mr. and Mrs. Billy Whiskers! Isn't it lovely that the Spots are going to give a party for you?" said Mrs. Wire Hair, one of the goats. "But I am in despair. Just look at my hair! It is all stained with yellow clay. And worse than that, with black muck, too. I nearly stranded in the quagmire down by the pond yesterday and now I am a sight!"

"None of us looks particularly well," said another. "What say you we have a swimming party and all go down to the brook and stand in the water until the stain and dirt is washed off?" said Billy Whiskers.

Billy Whiskers at Home

"A splendid idea! We knew if we came to you, Mr. Whiskers, you would think of some way we could look respectable at the party."

In less than half an hour, had you stood on the brow of the hill in the Watson barnyard and gazed down into the valley, you would have seen cows, horses, pigs, goats and sheep all standing in the pond into which the stream widened. Every animal had a happy face, for was not the water washing off the grime in fine shape? Billy's and Nannie's long white hair would soon look like spun silk. As for Button, he sat on a flat rock on the bank and licked his fur until it shone as if made of black satin.

All this time what do you suppose those mischievous Twins were doing but helping the Spots family carry things to eat down to the pasture where the party was to be? There was a shock of fresh green cornstalks in the Spots barnyard and this delicacy Mr. and Mrs. Spots, their children and several horses and cows were pulling out of the shock and carrying in their mouths down by the stream where the party was to be given. If the Twins had been asked to do this at home, they would have carried one mouthful and then complained that their legs were weary with climbing the hill. But to do it for other people was fun, and they never complained once, nor stopped until Mrs. Spots said they would not dare to carry away any more or it would be missed by Mr. Smith when he came into the barnyard.

Billy Whiskers at Home

As it was, Mr. Smith did wonder why it was so many of his horses, cows and pigs stayed in the barnyard that morning instead of going out into the pasture to eat the nice fresh clover. But finally he passed it by, thinking they just happened to remain as in all probability they had come in from the pasture to get a drink of nice cool water at the trough by the pump.

"I feel sick to my stomach, Punch. Let's go home," said Judy.

"Oh, no! You will feel better in a few minutes. You have been eating too many of those luscious green cornstalks. They act on goats just as too much candy acts on children. Go over and lie down on that nice soft turf by the haystack. Keep in the warm sun for a while and then if you do not feel better, I will take you home."

"Come," said one of the other goats, "let's go over with Judy and tell stories. My legs ache from going up and down that hill so many times carrying those cornstalks that I can scarcely stand. Besides, it will not be so lonesome for her and she will forget she feels ill."

When they were all lying down in a wide circle around Judy, Jill, one of Mrs. Spots' twins, said, "Now Punch, you tell the first story for it will be an interesting one, 'cause you can tell us one you have heard from Grandfather Whiskers."

"Oh, yes, do!" exclaimed Jack, the other twin.

"Oh, no," replied Punch. "I am tired of hearing him tell the

41

same ones over and over again to the different animals that call. You two tell stories instead."

"But we do not know any interesting ones!" they objected.

"Go ahead, Punch, and tell them about the time Grandfather went up in a hydroplane over the city of Rio de Janeiro in South America," urged Judy.

"Yes, do, do! That will be most exciting!" they all exclaimed.

So Punch began and their eyes were almost popping out of their heads at the thrilling experiences he was relating when they were nearly frightened out of their skins by a big cross dog running around the barn and suddenly appearing before them. For a moment he was as much surprised as they, for he had just come in with a farmer and was exploring things, as he had never been on this farm before. But in a minute he recovered himself and with a bark and a leap he landed in their midst. Such a hurrying and a scurrying as there was! Judy forgot she was ill and tried to climb up the haystack, steep as it was, but fell over backward, landing on the dog, frightening one as much as the other for a moment. On seeing the dog standing beside Judy, Punch pitched on him, though he was afraid of big dogs. But he had been taught he must always protect Judy, as she was a girl. Now Punch had short baby horns, but they could hurt, and the first thing this great dog knew, two sharp horns were running into his side. He turned with a snarl, ready to bite whatever it was

Billy Whiskers at Home

that was hurting him so, when lo! at that second a red cow with long, sharp horns came around the corner of the barn and seeing Punch about to be attacked by a strange dog, she gave one jump forward and

the next thing that dog knew, he was going up in the air at the rate of thirty-five miles an hour. He thought he was never coming down, but at last he did, though to his dismay he landed on top of a shed.

One of the little white calves that had been listening to Punch's story was so panic-stricken that she fled, but instead of keeping her eyes open to see where she was going, she shut them tight. The consequence was she fell headfirst into a tub of red dye and when she stood up she was no longer a snow-white calf but a brilliant red one.

Another calf was so frightened that she ran straight into the farmhouse kitchen and fell down the cellar stairs. The cook, who heard the commotion, came to see who was stamping around on her freshly scrubbed floor. But she saw no one, though she did hear a groan of pain down in the cellar.

"Who is there?" she called.

No answer—just a groan came from below.

She peered down the stairs, but no one was visible in the pitch black of the cellar. At last the cook gathered up courage enough to light a candle and go down two or three steps.

On seeing the light, the calf was so frightened she forgot her pain and went rushing around the cellar, stumbling over and upsetting everything. All the cook saw was a big red monster with glaring eyes. She dropped the candle in her fright and fled. Out the kitchen door she went, loudly calling for help. In a jiffy Mr. Smith and the farmer whose dog had made all this trouble came running to discover the cause of the commotion.

"There is something awful in the cellar! All hair and eyes! And it is running around upsetting everything!" she said.

Billy Whiskers at Home

"Wait until I get a pitchfork to drive it out, and I will see what it is. Light a lantern for me," Mr. Smith commanded.

With a pitchfork in one hand and a lantern in the other, Mr. Smith started down the cellar stairs with the neighbor farmer close behind him brandishing a long whip in one hand and holding his dog by the collar with the other.

The dog quickly smelt the calf, gave a jerk and down the stairs he bounded, knocking the lantern out of Mr. Smith's hand, putting out the light and smashing the chimney. Then the hubbub began. The dog chased the calf around the cellar, giving her nips every once in a while that made the poor frightened beast bellow. At last the calf made for the stairs. Seeing a big red animal with blazing eyes come out of the darkness, the two farmers turned and fled. But the animal came after them, followed by the dog. When they were out in the light of day, Mr. Smith saw it was only a calf, but a very queer calf. By this time the calf was standing on the kitchen table right in the midst of the luncheon dishes. She had been so terrified by the dog that she had jumped on a chair and from there to the table. The dog was barking furiously and trying to get up on the table too.

"Get out of here! You have made enough trouble for one day!" and the farmer grabbed his dog by the collar and dragged him out. Indeed, he literally had to drag him away from the calf. He whined and made a terrific fuss as he was dragged along, and it was only by tying him to the back of the wagon that his owner took him away.

The moment the Twins saw the dog disappear into the house they had cut sticks for home, and never stopped running until they came to the pond where their father and mother and all the rest of the Watson farm animals were standing in the water.

"What are you all standing in the water for?" asked Punch.

"We are making ourselves clean for the party," answered their father. "But where have you been? You look as if you had been standing in a lake too, you are so wet with perspiration."

"Oh, we have been racing down the hill to see which could reach here first," easily replied Punch.

"Well, you better lie down in the shade and cool off. Don't you dare come into this cold pond until you are perfectly dry. If you do, both of you may have chills."

So off the Twins walked and lay down under a tree to watch the other animals. "My, Punch, but that was an awful scare! He frightened me so I am still trembling," confessed Judy.

CHAPTER V

THE "WELCOME HOME" PARTY

T last it was nearly time to start for the party. The only thing there was to wait for now was for Mr. and Mrs. Watson to go to bed, as it would never do for the animals to start and then have Mr. Watson come out to the barn and discover them all gone.

To-night of all nights it seemed as if he would never turn out the lights. All eyes in the barnyard were watching the living-room, waiting for the lights there to be turned out and for those in the bedroom to be switched on. The window shades were up and the animals could see Mr. Watson comfortably seated in his big armchair reading the evening paper, his wife near him busy with her knitting.

"Oh!" exclaimed one of the young heifers, "I am growing so nervous waiting I could kick down the barn doors! It is such a glorious evening I want to start early and stay late."

"There," said another cow, "he has gone out to the pump to get his last glass of cold water before retiring, for I can hear the old pump handle squeak. But oh, dear me, he is sitting down again! He

47

Billy Whiskers at Home

never does that! He always goes to bed directly after he drinks his glass of water."

"See, Mrs. Watson is holding up the sock she is knitting and she is pointing to the toe. I believe she is asking him to wait until she finishes it. Yes, that is surely what she has done, for he is taking up his paper again," remarked a third.

"I shall just die," said the young heifer, "if they do not soon go to bed and let us get off. There are so many of us, why couldn't some of us go on ahead? Then if he comes out, there would be plenty left and he would not miss those who have gone."

This was being discussed when oh, joy! the lights in the living-room went out and those upstairs flashed on. A minute after that the procession, Billy at its head, moved silently but quickly out of the barnyard and down the hill to the little stream in the meadow which they followed until it brought them to Mr. Smith's farm as this was the same little brook that wandered through Mr. Smith's pasture where the party was to be held.

First came Billy and Nannie, then Billy Junior and Daisy, and then followed in pairs the pigs, sheep, young cattle, old cows and horses last. In this way the shortest went first and each could see over the heads of the animals in front of them. You never saw such a clean, glossy lot of animals as every one of them had spent most of the day in cleaning and shining their coats, either by taking a bath

Billy Whiskers at Home

in the brook or rolling in the sand. Then to make themselves smell sweet, they had rolled in the mint bed by the stream or else crushed the sweet smelling garden pinks that had boldly pushed their heads through the garden fence.

They had gone about half their way when in the dim light they saw Farmer Jones' cattle hurrying helter skelter in their direction, likewise bound for the party. They were coming in no regular order at all. First one would be ahead and then another. And their coats looked mussed and dirty. One white cow had great chunks of mud clinging to her sides.

When the Jones cattle saw how beautifully clean and spick and span the Watson animals looked, they were so ashamed of their own appearance that they felt like going home, and, in fact, the white cow did go back and clean up, arriving much later. She could not face the glossy cattle while she was in such a mess.

The leader of the Jones cattle was an old, old cow, and when she came up to Billy and saw how fine his procession looked, she gave a deep sigh and said, "I

Billy Whiskers at Home

never thought of asking my cattle to clean up or to form into a procession, and here we come to the party looking just as we do every day. My, oh my! I can't tell you how mortified I feel! But I assure you I never thought of cleaning up or of marching over in a dignified way instead of all rushing along pell-mell. But then you are young and up-to-date while I am old and set in my ways and how I am going to look never enters my head. I guess I am too old to be the leader of young stock and I shall resign my place to-morrow. Do you think we would have time to clean up a bit before we go to the party?" she inquired anxiously.

"Certainly! There is lots of time. Just go down to the brook and wade in it a little while and you will even then have ample time to get to the party before it is late. We came early because the younger cattle were so impatient to be off that I consented to an early start," said Billy.

"Thank you so much, Mr. Whiskers, for your kind advice. I shall take it, and when we appear at the party at least we shall have the dust and dirt washed out of our hair, even if we do not shine like all of you. We won't have time to let our hair dry and lick it down. What is more, when we do arrive, we will come in some sort of order, and not all helter skelter," and she walked off to issue instructions covering what she planned to do.

She really expected to have a great deal of trouble in persuading her cattle to stop to clean themselves. But not so; they were every one glad to do so as they saw what a sorry sight they made compared to Billy's procession.

When Billy arrived, he took his stand beside Mr. and Mrs. Spots, who were receiving under an old gnarled weeping willow tree beside the stream. He then presented to Mr. and Mrs. Spots those of his animals who had never met their host and hostess, after which the procession broke rank and wandered at will in little groups, mingling with the animals from the other farms. It was a very large party—the largest by far ever given by animals in these parts.

About half an hour after Billy's group arrived, the Jones cattle came, and you never saw such a difference in appearance in the way they looked now and in the meadow.

The animals were having a most enjoyable time when suddenly they heard the most distressing baaing and groaning down in the meadow, but coming nearer and nearer as if the animal was running. As they listened, they could distinguish the words "Mama, mama, save us, save us!" Daisy pricked up her ears and recognizing the voices, she was off with a bound. Her husband followed, and Billy Whiskers too.

"What ever can be the trouble?" said Nannie. "The Twins wanted to come with us, but of course we would not permit that. Probably they have followed us and been frightened by something."

Billy Whiskers at Home

That is just what it proved to be. The Twins grew lonesome after their father, mother, grandfather and grandmother and all the farm animals had departed, so they decided to follow them but keep out of sight when they reached the party. But when they were in the meadow where the grass grew away over their heads, they became frightened and were debating whether or not to go back home when with a bound there came a wolf out of the tall grass. Now if there is one thing a goat fears more than all else, it is a wolf.

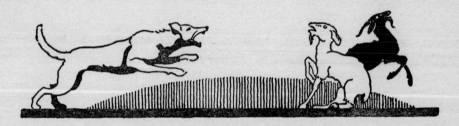

The Twins let out a wild baa and began to run like mad toward the party, where they knew they would gain safety. As they ran they could feel the hot breath of the wolf and they were about to drop in sheer fright and exhaustion from running and crying when just before them they saw their grandfather, father and mother. With one bound Billy was beside them, ready to kill the grey wolf he saw close behind them. But when he looked a second time, instead of a wolf, he saw a neighbor's big grey dog. He was also coming to the party and the Twins in their fright had mistaken him for a wolf.

Daisy was determined to take the Twins right back home, but Mr. and Mrs. Spots insisted that she put them to bed with their children in the stable, where they could sleep in safety until the party was over. This was finally agreed upon, and when everything was quiet again, Billy was asked to give them a talk about his travels.

CHAPTER VI

THE BRAZILIAN BULL FIGHT

FTER the calling of "Speech! A speech from Billy Whiskers!" had died down some, Billy climbed up to a shelf of rock that protruded from the brow of a hill overlooking the lower stretch of land where the party was in progress. From this vantage point he could be seen and heard by all. The moment he stepped forward and began to speak, there was dead silence and not a horse or cow so much as switched its tail to chase away the flies.

"My dear friends, it gives me great pleasure to be back in your midst once more, and to have the opportunity to see and speak to you. My very dear and old friends, Mr. and Mrs. Spots, who have made it possible for me to meet you all this evening, have asked me to relate one or two of the experiences I had while away. I can assure you I have had many thrilling ones. But instead of telling you about them, I am going to describe one of the most peculiar sights I saw while in South America.

"As you well know, wherever a country has been settled by the Spanish or the Portuguese, there bull fights have been introduced, as it is the national sport of those two countries. Consequently when I was in Rio de Janeiro and heard people talking about going to the bull fight on Sunday afternoon (they are always held on Sunday) I decided to see what they were like, though I did not relish the idea in the least as I dislike to see any kind of an animal hurt or abused. You see I had heard that a bull fight is one of the most cruel sports engaged in by any nation. Still I felt that as long as I was in a country where they had them, I had better go and see how they are conducted and what the people who attend these fights look like. If I found it too cruel, I could come away.

"I followed the crowd going to the bull ring, and succeeded in slipping in between the people and finding a good place away up on the last tier of seats from which to witness the fight.

"I had been there only a few minutes when with a blare of trumpets a pair of double doors was thrown open and out rode a toreador on a coal black horse prancing in time to the music as he champed his bit while his rider bowed low to the audience. Before him as he pranced around the ring went two trumpeters dressed in red velvet and silver lace, blaring away on their extra long beribboned trumpets. As for the toreador, he was costumed in black velvet and gold lace, and wore a three-cornered hat with a long flowing white ostrich plume, and carried a long spear

Billy Whiskers at Home

held upright. Behind him marched the picadores and matadores.

After this company once circles the ring, it is the custom for the toreador to take his place in the middle of the ring, facing the door through which the bulls enter the ring from their partially darkened stalls. The door from the stall into the ring is thrown wide open and seeing the bright light, the bull rushes for it, so that when he first enters the ring he is blinded by the sudden glare, and he stands, head erect, looking in all directions, puzzled which way to turn.

"The first bull to enter on the day I was there was a magnificent jet black beast with long, pointed horns, though the points had been sawed off, as that is the law in Brazil. Also no horse or bull may be killed or injured. The toreador, picadores and matadores are there to protect the horse and to keep him from being disemboweled or injured in any way. They are permitted to tease the bull and throw long darts into the bull but not to injure him.

"When I found this out I was delighted for now I could enjoy watching the fight and let my nerves quiet down.

"As soon as the bull's eyes were accustomed to the light, he spied the toreador on the horse facing him, and with a snort he began to paw the dirt and switch his tail. He charged on horse and man but he was not quick enough. The horse jumped to one side and

Billy Whiskers at Home

the toreador threw a dart that sank into the bull's hind quarter. With a quick turn the bull was after them again and for some little time they chased each other here, there and everywhere around the ring until the toreador had thrown another dart into him.

"While the toreador was trying to make the darts stick in the

bull's shoulders or haunches, the picadores teased him by shaking a red cape in his face or else throwing it in front of him just when he was about to gore the horse. The bull took after the picadores and they had to run for safety, jumping over a medium high wall that surrounded the whole ring, and formed a very narrow passageway. It was built just high enough for a bull that is a good jumper to get over, but the passageway was so narrow that if he went over straight, there was not sufficient room

Billy Whiskers at Home

for the bull. This bull hung over the wall until he could twist himself straight, which delay gave the picadores time to escape and they returned to the ring. This happened many times that day and made the audience howl with delight and clap their hands. As soon as the bull would get himself straightened out, he would run around

the enclosure until he came to an open door, and running through it he would find himself in the ring once again.

"This performance continued with each bull until he would have two darts sticking in him and then another bull was brought on, and this one was led out by six cream-colored oxen with humps on their backs like water buffalo have. These oxen were trained to walk over to where the bull stood and quietly encircle him, so that he walked out in the midst of friends.

"As many as eight or nine bulls were used in that one afternoon. Some of them would not fight at all, even though stuck with sharp darts and annoyed in every imaginable way. When one refused to fight, it was led out by the cream-colored oxen and another bull brought in.

"The performance was concluded with a kind of burlesque show such as one might see at a circus. Two men dressed in suits made of thick rubber like automobile tires came into the ring. They were so clumsy in their suits they could scarcely waddle, and when a bull knocked them over, he could not hurt them. When they fell and he rolled them around, they simply pulled their heads into the suits much as a tortoise pulls its head into its shell, and let the bull maul them until he was driven off by the picadores. Then the picadores would help them to their feet as their suits made them so clumsy they could not get up if once they fell down.

"These men made the bulls furious. They bellowed and stamped and swished their tails with anger, all of which tickled the crowd immensely.

"Another thing they had that greatly pleased the audience was a paper ship under full sail. Four men got inside the ship and carried it around. It was a comical sight as the men's legs showed

Billy Whiskers at Home

below the ship where the water ought to be. They stood where the bull would see the ship the first thing on entering the ring. At first the bull was so astonished he simply stood still and stared at them. Then with a swish of his tail, he made for it at full speed. A single onslaught shattered it and there was a grand melee of bull, men's legs, sails and splinters. The bull was all tangled up in the sails, and while he was trying to extricate himself, a man on stilts and dressed in a long Mother Hubbard and wearing a false face of Mother Hubbard and that good lady's bonnet walked into the ring. For a while Mother Hubbard dodged the bull cleverly, but at last she stumbled and fell across the bull's back. When the bull finally freed himself of his burden, the false face with the bonnet was still sticking between his horns, the dress and stilts trailing across his broad back, while the man impersonating Mother Hubbard was running for shelter back into the bull shed.

"This was the last performance of the day and it sent the crowd home laughing instead of horrified as a real bull fight would have done. And I for one say that all bull fights should be like this one and no government should be permitted to hold such cruel and horrible ones as are given in Spanish countries."

Billy bowed low in conclusion and was about to leave the jutting rock he had used as a platform when the crowd of animals below cried, "Tell us something more! Tell us something more! We never travel nor see anything of the world, and it will be the greatest treat for us if you will tell us what you saw and did."

So Billy walked back to his place and proceeded to relate how he had personified King Neptune.

CHAPTER VII

BILLY PERSONIFIES NEPTUNE

"THIS adventure took place while I was on the good ship *Vandyck* bound for South America," began Billy. "As the ship neared the equator, there was great excitement on board for a fancy dress ball was being planned to welcome King Neptune when he boarded the ship as we glided over the equator.

"Those of the passengers who had brought no fancy costumes with them had to improvise them out of things they had and by the help of borrowed finery, for at such a time travelers are more than willing to loan anything they possess to help piece out the costume of a fellow-passenger. Especially was this true on board the *Vandyck*, as prizes were to be given for the best costume made on board, and another for the costume truest to type, while honorable mention was promised to that person wearing the handsomest costume.

"The ball was at its height when the ship's bells rang out the hour of midnight, the dance was stopped and all eyes were turned toward the side of the ship over which Neptune was to appear and claim his throne. Then all the passengers were to walk before him and be presented by the court officials dressed in full court regalia. After the presentation, games were to be played and feats of skill performed before King Neptune for his amusement, after which refreshments were to be served and the gayety and dancing kept up until very late.

"Generally one of the ship's officers takes the part of Neptune, for you must know this ball is held on every trip the ship makes to South America. And very fine does he look with snow-white hair and flowing beard and long purple velvet robe with its ermine cape, to say nothing of the golden crown and all the other regalia of a really truly king, even to the golden staff tipped with Neptune's trident.

"But on this trip the officers had conceived the idea of dressing me up as king and seating me on the throne, as I have been trained to sit up and hold my fore legs down like arms. So the night the ball was in progress, the officers seated me on the throne while the guests were dancing. Once seated, they hurriedly draped the royal purple robe around me, fitted the golden crown on my head to hide my horns, tied the staff to my left leg which I rested on the arm of the golden chair of state, stuck a monocle in one eye, and as the ship's bells ceased ringing at midnight, a page with a silver trumpet marched to the side of the ship where the guests were dancing and led the way to King Neptune's throne, where they were presented.

SEEING MR. ROBINSON DANGLING THERE, BILLY GAVE HIM A MIGHTY
BUTT THAT SHOVED HIM ALL THE WAY THROUGH.

(Page 95)

Billy Whiskers at Home

When the passengers raised their heads after the deep ceremonial bow of presentation, each one was impressed by a weirdness in King Neptune's appearance. The more they gazed, the more pronounced was the strangeness. What could it be? There was the long white hair and beard, but the eyes had a peculiar twinkle in them and the nose was exceedingly broad. Why did the king look so different from all other times they had seen him? This was Neptune. Yet it was not the Neptune they had expected to see. But they could not tarry in front of him and stare while in a procession, for after their ceremonial bow they must move on, giving place to others.

"Once they had passed by the throne, the passengers quickly gathered in groups to discuss the queer looking Neptune. Every

Billy Whiskers at Home

one had been presented when a great clatter was heard. Neptune had dropped his staff, and the next thing they knew, they were gazing at the unusual spectacle of a king running on all fours from his throne, and as they looked, they saw him approach the side of the ship and plunge over its side.

"It was not the ocean into which I, King Neptune, leaped but only the swimming tank at the ship's side, just under the promenade deck, but they said afterward it looked exactly as if the king had jumped into the ocean. Every one ran to that side of the ship, expecting to see the king rising and falling on the billows but no king could they see. Had they watched the swimming tank, they would have seen a goat being divested of his robes and crown by five or six sailors who were try-

66

ing to save me from drowning, as I had become so entangled in my robes I could not swim. All the while the sailors were trying to keep me from drowning, other sailors were letting out the water as fast as it could be drained from the tank.

"It was some time before the excited passengers could return to their dancing and march before the judges but it was finally accomplished. They decided that the prettiest costume was worn by a sweet young girl representing a pink rosebud. The overskirts of her dress formed the petals of the rose, and she wore a wreath of buds in her sunny gold hair. The most handsome costume was that of a tall, stately brunette who appeared as the Queen of Sheba. Her garments had been brought from Egypt. The best outfit made from things picked up on board was a Turkish lady of the harem. She wore changeable yellow silk bloomers loaned by one of the ladies coming back from Turkey. Over them she wore a rainbow tinted scarf tied as a sash, with a crimson velvet jacket over a blouse with flowing white silk sleeves embroidered in gold, while over her head was thrown a pale silver-blue veil, thin and airy as a cloud, held in place by a gold band worn low on her forehead. On neck, wrists and ankles tinkled gold coins, while on her feet she wore bright red morocco slippers with sharp-pointed toes. She made a perfect favorite of the harem. The most original costume was fashioned entirely of newspapers and was called 'current events.'

Billy Whiskers at Home

"They said the only drawback to the whole evening's performance was the loss of Neptune's robe which I had ruined by jumping into the water. But when the passengers found out that it was their old pet Billy Whiskers who had impersonated King Neptune, they thought it was so clever of me to sit on the throne for so long decked out in all that finery that they did not blame me for running away. They took up a collection to buy a new robe in the place of the one the water had ruined, and so, my friends, no harm came of the unusual evening.

"When I went down below to my quarters where all the animals belonging to the passengers were kept, they gathered around me to hear what had taken place.

" 'Tell you what, Bill,' said an English bulldog, 'you did make a bully good looking king. Really in your royal robes you did not look unlike King George—and I have seen King George and know what I am talking about.'

" 'But what made you jump into the swimming tank?' asked a French poodle.

" 'For the moment I forgot it was there,' I explained, 'and I ached so from sitting up so long that I thought my back would break. Then, too, the crown was cutting into my head, and I was half smothered with that fur cape and all the rest of the things I wore.'

" 'It is a good thing we saw them dress you up in the afternoon to

68

Billy Whiskers at Home

find how the things were going to fit you,' said another dog, 'or we would never have gotten a peep at you, for they shut us in at sundown and you did not appear until midnight.'

"That is the whole story," concluded Billy, bowing left and right, and stepping down from the rocky ledge he had used as a platform.

Now it was Stubby's turn to tell of his experiences.

CHAPTER VIII

STUBBY RELATES HIS EXPERIENCE WITH SEALS

STUBBY looked only as big as a minute as he mounted the rock to recount his experience.

"The most thrilling and exciting adventure I had while we were in California was at the Catalina Islands, where we went to ride in the glass-bottomed rowboats they have there so people may see the bottom of the ocean and get a peek at the sea feathers, coral, flowers and fish. What one sees through the clear water is most beautiful. Little hills and hollows of the purest yellow or white sand, with long, dull pink swaying plants resembling ostrich plumes growing out of it. Next to them there may be bright yellow fan-shaped plants around the roots of which is white and pink coral exactly the shape of a man's brains, or else in the form of sprays. And from these same mounds of glistening golden sand will bloom the delicate waxy sea anemones. Oh, it is most enchanting, and one expects to see a mermaid glide through this sea garden along with the gold, blue and silver fish that swim among these plants as our birds fly through our trees.

Billy Whiskers at Home

"Then if one wishes to row out about a mile where the water is so deep the bottom cannot be seen, they find the shoals of bluefish. That is a wonderful treat, for here they will see hundreds of young bluefish from six to twelve inches long, all facing in the same direction, apparently resting on the long-stemmed plants that grow up from the bottom of the ocean and have little yellow balloons on the stems to keep them from falling back. This is one of the feeding places of the bluefish where they stay when the tide is running out and eat the particles of sea food it washes out to them. All the fish face one way, there being tiers of fish, one on top of the other, with only a few inches between each tier as far down in the ocean as one can see.

"The queerest part of it is that they keep their fins moving in and out but do not move or swim about at all. They are as blue as the bluest sky you ever saw and they make a wonderfully beautiful picture.

"As one approaches these bluefish banks, as they are called, the reflection of their color makes the water above them turn a dark shade so the fishermen can tell by the color of the water where they are feeding.

"You will say there is nothing thrilling about this peaceful scene," said Stubby. "But wait! I am coming to that. I just had to tell you about this most exquisite sight.

Billy Whiskers at Home

"Well, when we came back from our ride in the little rowboat, a man on the dock was calling out, 'Right this way for the glass-bottomed steamer that takes you to the Seal Rocks! You see the seals at home and the way they live. All the way there you can gaze through the glass bottom and see the wonderful Sea Garden. At a point where it is most beautiful a man in a diver's suit will enter the water and bring to you any flower or shell you may wish. Starting in ten minutes, returning in one hour for the small price of one dollar. Don't miss seeing this wonder garden of the deep!'

"It all sounded good to me, so I went on board and prepared to gaze at the same beauties I had seen in the rowboat, but when we started I was very much disappointed to see instead of the exquisitely colored fish, flowers and swaying plants just a few unattractive shells, and no flowers or feathers at all. And when the diver went overboard there was nothing attractive for him to get to bring back. I heard one of the passengers say that he had taken this trip years ago and that then there were sea feathers and plants and coral but that all the years people had been carrying them away until now scarcely anything was left. What we did see were put there from time to time, so the diver could have something to bring the people, charging twenty-five cents for each piece he brought. So I stopped gazing through the glass bottom and went to the side of the boat where I could watch the antics of a mother seal and two or three

Billy Whiskers at Home

others. The boat seemed to make them very angry, and the mother seal appeared to be trying to stop it or frighten it away, for she kept up a constant crying and approached nearer and nearer the boat as if she wished to bite it.

"I heard the captain tell a lady the seal made such a fuss because she was trying to frighten the boat so it would not go to her home

on Seal Rock; that possibly she had a baby there that she had left behind while she went out to look for food.

"'When we round that point you see ahead, you will hear the most awful racket set up for all the seals will begin to bark. The males will dive and leap out of the water and come toward us, swimming round and round the ship and under us all the time we are at the Rocks, for this is where they live and breed. Do you see that

74

Billy Whiskers at Home

big, dark object on the top of that large rock projecting out into the sea? Well, watch it closely and you will see it is a seal. He is their leader and he always stays out there where he can catch the first glimpse of any intruder and give the alarm. He is by far the oldest and largest seal in these waters. There are now many young seals on the island, which makes him more fierce than usual for the male seals look after their families well and try to protect them from all danger.

" 'There, he has spied us and given alarm! When we turn that point of land he is on we will be facing a curved rocky beach and on those rocks you will see hundreds and hundreds of seals of all ages and colors, for the baby seals are cream colored, while the older seals have dark brown coats.'

"True to all the captain said, the moment we rounded the point, one would have thought bedlam had been turned loose, for every seal was barking—the old seals loudly and fiercely, the baby seals with mere squeaks.

"I left the captain and went to the side of the ship to watch the seals slip off the high rocks into the water and come toward us with that peculiar gliding motion seals alone have. In a few minutes there were hundreds of them around our boat. I was standing by a little eight-year-old boy, my fore paws on the rail of the boat, when, horror of horrors! I felt him give me a push and into that seething

75

Billy Whiskers at Home

mass of angry seals I went head first. I thought my time had come, and that I would be eaten alive, the seals looked so fierce. They swam under me, tossing me three or four feet up in the air. They swam over me, sending me almost to the very bottom of the ocean. Then again they would swim around me, twirling me around so fast it made my head swim. Every minute I expected to have them bite me. When I came to the surface after one of those times when they had pushed me down to the bottom, I heard the boat's whistle tooting like mad and I realized that the captain was doing it to

frighten the seals away. It served the purpose, too, for it did that very thing, every one of the seals quickly making for the shore. As soon as they had left me, I swam toward the boat and the captain lowered a bushel basket tied to a rope for me to crawl in, which I did and then a sailor pulled me quickly to the deck. Since that day

Billy Whiskers at Home

I have never wanted to see a seal and when I chance to walk through a park and hear them barking, it makes the cold shivers run up and down my spine to think what I endured while those seals were surrounding me."

Stubby's experience pleased the crowd greatly, and they showed their appreciation by stamping their feet on the ground and bellowing, grunting, barking, meowing, baaing and bleating.

Amidst this applause Stubby left the platform.

CHAPTER IX

BUTTON IS SPEAKER

FTER Stubby had spoken, it was Button's turn to tell what had befallen him.

"If you animals will excuse me, I shall be greatly obliged, as I am no speaker and nothing of interest has happened to me for a long time," he said.

"Oh, yes, there has! I know there has!" said Billy. "Go ahead and tell them what happened to you at the Barbados!"

"Yes, do," Stubby agreed. "That *was* an extremely exciting experience."

So Button mounted the rocky ledge and began:

"Our ship had anchored about two miles out in the roadstead, and every one was on deck waiting for the little rowboats to come to take them ashore. The water is not deep enough at the wharf for sea-going vessels to dock. As they waited, the passengers were hanging over the rail watching the little negro boys dive for coins down into the deep, deep waters where sharks and swordfish lurk

79

Billy Whiskers at Home

awaiting a chance to bite off an arm or leg or run a long sword into the body of an unwary swimmer.

"A man and his wife in a rowboat came up close to the ship to display their wares. They had a lovely parrot in one cage and another full of red, yellow and vari-colored birds for sale, and also jewelry cleverly fashioned out of shells, and handbags made of the brown, glossy reeds of a plant that grows on the island. I was watching the pair when quick as a wink a man pushed me off the ship's rail where I was curled up to view all that went on beneath me.

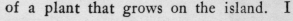

"My surprise was so great when I found myself falling from the height of the promenade deck that I could not think, and when I landed in the woman's lap in the rowboat, I would have leaped overboard had she not held on to me.

"The man who had pushed me overboard called out, 'The cat for

BILLY SURPRISED AUGUSTA BY BUTTING HER RIGHT OVER HIS HEAD,
AND SHE LANDED IN THE TROUGH WITH A GREAT SPLASH.

(PAGE 113)

Billy Whiskers at Home

a parrot! That cat is a valuable one but I will part with him for your talking parrot.'

"To his surprise, the woman quickly agreed to the trade and tied the parrot's cage to a rope that was let down. The cage had just reached the deck level and the man was untying it when I spied it as it was loosened and swung in the woman's lap. With a bound I grabbed it and began to climb up. The woman's husband stretched out his hand to stop me but he was too late. I had climbed too high for him to reach me and in trying to do so he came near upsetting his boat with all his wares and his wife in it. Indeed, had it not been for the woman's presence of mind to throw her whole weight to the opposite side of the boat, it would surely have capsized.

"When I reached the top of the rope, the man who had thrown me overboard tried to prevent me from coming on deck by pushing my head back. But at last I wearied of having him treat me so, and the next time he touched me I reached out one paw and gave him a scratch that quickly made him let go the rope. While he was nursing his hand and too engrossed with the pain to think of what I was doing, I jumped aboard and ran into the saloon. As I went, I heard the boatman and his wife calling loudly to the man on board to send back their parrot or pay them for it. After tormenting them for some time by pretending he was going to keep the parrot, he wrapped some money in a paper and threw it into their boat.

Billy Whiskers at Home

"I considered it a narrow escape for I would not have lived with that couple for worlds. There is no country, no matter how beautiful, where I have ever been or about which I have ever heard in which I should like to live but the United States of America.

"Well, as time went on, the man who bought the parrot neglected her so, forgetting to feed her and give her water to drink and for her bath that I felt sorry for her and I told her that when we stopped at the Island of Trinidad I would open her cage door and let her out if she thought she could fly ashore and take care of herself after she had gained land.

Billy Whiskers at Home

" 'Of course I can, for my wings have never been clipped and on that island grows every kind of food I need, just as in the Barbados.'

" 'Very well, then, I will open your cage door and free you,' I promised.

"Consequently when we reached Trinidad, I wiggled and fussed with her cage door until I succeeded in opening it. Then I had the pleasure of seeing her fly for the shore, where she alighted on the top of a tall cocoanut palm tree. How I did enjoy her owner's discomfiture when he discovered she was gone! He made a great fuss and said his bird had been stolen and insisted the entire ship be searched for her, though one of the sailors said he had seen a green parrot fly to shore shortly after we had landed. He declared parrots are clever birds and said she probably loosed the door with her bill and squeezed herself out, as he had seen them do that trick before."

The crowd cheered and cheered in the usual way and said they wished Button would tell them another experience. But he hurried off the rock platform and lost himself in the crowd so they could not press him to tell another.

CHAPTER X

BILLY RUNS AWAY

ALL the next day the animals and fowls too listened with all their ears to discover whether or not Mr. Watson or any of the farm hands knew they had been away at a party the night before. But not a word was spoken about it so they decided no one thought they had been off the farm.

"My, didn't we have a good time? One to be remembered all our lives! And Father Billy's talk was most entertaining," said Daisy.

"We certainly did, and the Chums related such thrilling things that it would almost pay to let them go traveling again so they could have some more unusual experiences to relate when they came home," agreed her husband.

"Oh, hi there, Billy Whiskers, where are you?" called Mr. Watson. "I want you to pull Ruthie to town in the little goat cart. She is going in to spend the day with some little friends, and they wish to have a ride in her cart."

85

Billy Whiskers at Home

So the new harness with all the shining silver buckles on it was put on Billy and he was hitched to the cunning little cart and away drove Ruthie, Mr. Watson's little four-year-old granddaughter who had come to the farm for a visit with her mother, the only daughter of Mr. and Mrs. Watson.

Billy trotted along the road almost as fast as a pony would go, for the cart and Ruthie were a light burden for such a big, strong goat, and it was no time until they were in town. Of course Mr. Watson drove a little way behind them so he could be ready to take a hand should any accident occur in case they met a drove of cattle, for he did not know what Billy might do in such an emergency.

Billy Whiskers at Home

The first thing they did on coming to the town was to go straight to the home of Grace, the little girl Ruthie was to visit. There they piled into the cart all the children the little wagon could hold, and took them for a nice long ride around town, returning just before luncheon. Before they went into the house they unhitched Billy and gave him just what he liked best to eat: carrots and a bunch of sweet hay with a big pail of cold well water to drink. Then they left him to wander around in the big yard as he pleased, taking care that all the gates were tightly shut before they left him.

Billy ate his dinner which he enjoyed greatly, being extremely hungry after pulling the children all about the town. After he had eaten, he sought the shade of a big tree and took a nap. He awoke feeling very much refreshed and hearing the children laughing at their play on the other side of the house, he thought this would be a good time to run off and hide before they tired of the swing and came for him to take them for another ride. This he had determined he would not do, having ahead of him the long pull to take Ruthie back to the farm.

As you know, gates were nothing to Billy when he wished to go somewhere, as he could jump any gate he ever saw. With a bound now he was over one and out on the street, running as fast as ever he could go toward Lake Winnebago which he could see rippling in the distance.

87

Billy Whiskers at Home

On his arrival at the shore of the lake, feeling hot and dusty from pulling the little cart around during the morning, he decided to go for a swim. This he enjoyed, coming out greatly refreshed and rested. While he was shaking himself dry, up the beach he spied a queer looking object. He could not make out what it was, so he determined to run up and find out. He had almost reached the spot when something glided on top of the water for a short distance and then rose from the surface and flew for quite a distance as straight up in the air as ever it could go. Then it descended in graceful curves to the water, and again made a flight.

"Heigho! They are hydroplanes!" exclaimed Billy. "My, how I wish I could get a ride in one! I know I should just love the sensation of gliding on the water and then flying straight up in the air. I think I shall go as close as I can to them and see what they look like at close range."

When he arrived and saw one after the other of the planes make a flight, he was more anxious than ever to ride in one. At last he was so near he could have stepped off the platform one plane was lying against, and in fact was about to do so and take all chances when some boys discovered him and began to throw stones at him. He paid no attention to them, but thought how cruel and selfish boys could be to throw stones at him when he was not bothering any one, only looking at the fascinating planes just as they were.

Billy Whiskers at Home

But when they sicked two dogs on him, he knew he would have to go. They chased him to the end of the pier. He could go no farther unless he jumped into the water. Then when one of the dogs snapped at him, he turned to his tormentor and hooked him straight up in the air, and he came down inside one of the hydroplanes just as it was rising from the water, carrying him up with it. The dog was so afraid in the plane that he jumped out when they were about fifty feet in the air, and went kersplash in the water, disappearing from sight and probably touching the very bottom of the lake. When he came to the surface he swam for shore and, reaching it, cut sticks for home as fast as his long legs would carry him.

On seeing what had happened to his friend, the second dog slunk off and disappeared from sight, no one knew where.

Then some rough boys and men thought they would have some fun with Billy and walked out to the end of the pier to tease him, but after the first man had been butted into the lake, the others thought they would not try it. Seeing there was too large a crowd gathered on the

Billy Whiskers at Home

shore for him to make his way through it, Billy Whiskers leaped into the water, swimming near the shore until he was so far away that the crowd would not bother him any more. He landed and tried to find his way back to the house where Ruthie was visiting, for he knew by the position of the sun he must have been away a long time. But the more he tried to find the house, the more confused he grew. Billy Whiskers knew he was lost.

He ran up and down the streets, baaing as loudly as he could, hoping he might happen to pass the house and Ruthie would run out and bring him in. But no such luck attended him and his baaing only attracted the attention of the mischievous boys, who threw stones after him or chased him up and down one street after another. He had just escaped one group of boys and was quietly walking down a street, trying to recover his breath, when he heard the voices of several children in a yard the other side of a high stone wall. He thought he recognized Ruthie's voice, and ran to the gate and peeped in, but no, to his disappointment all the children were boys. They were acting so queerly he stopped to watch them for a minute or two, and then he discovered they were trying to do the tricks they had seen the clowns and trapeze performers do at the circus. He was so busy gazing at them that he pushed the gate open and went inside that he might have a close view of the hand springs and backward somersaults they were turning.

CHAPTER XI

AN EXCITING DAY FOR BILLY

AS Billy stood watching the antics of the boys, a bumble bee began buzzing around his head, bothering him by darting in and out of his ears. He shook his head and tried also to paw it away, but it still persisted in humming around and darting at him.

"Say, you old buzzer, if you don't keep away from me, I'll swallow you alive," threatened Billy.

Just then the bee made a dive for his nose, but Billy opened his mouth and swallowed it. But not before the bee had stung his tongue. The pain was terrific, and Billy jumped about as if he had suddenly gone crazy. He stood on his head, rolled in the grass, wheeled round and round on his hind legs and pawed the air with his fore feet, all the while bleating pitifully.

Seeing the goat carrying on in this way, the boys thought he was trying to mimic them, which made them laugh so they could not stand up, for of course they did not know he had been stung. Alas

Billy Whiskers at Home

for them! Billy thought they were making sport of his pain, and with a single bound he was upon them, glad of a chance to hurt something as he was being hurt. He kicked, butted and pawed them until he had sent one boy over the fence into the alley, and another was doubled up with his hands over his stomach. Two boys escaped, but the fifth ran toward the kitchen door, Billy in hot pursuit.

The boy had slammed the door in Billy's face and was running through the house when Billy butted a big hole straight through the screen door. This brought the goat up behind a big, fat cook who had her hands in bread dough. Before she knew what had happened, she felt herself falling backward. To save herself, she grabbed at the bread pan. Of course it slid off the table and she fell on the floor. The bread pan turned upside down over Billy's horns, and the sticky mass of dough went trickling down over one eye and on down over his nose.

Billy Whiskers at Home

The cook's screams brought the master of the house from his study to the kitchen, but on arriving at the doorway he was met by an infuriated goat who lowered his head to butt him. On seeing such an adversary, the master made haste to retreat and quickly put the dining table between them. But he was not quite nimble enough for Billy was close on his heels and the chase was on.

Round and round that table they ran, with Billy gaining at every step, Mr. Robinson calling loudly for help. Bridget had collected her wits by this time and came to his rescue with a broom and every time Billy passed her on his way around the table after Mr. Robinson, she gave him a whack with it. Billy paid not the slightest attention to her, as he was much too intent on overtaking Mr. Robinson and giving him one mighty butt. In an ill-fated moment Mr. Robinson's foot slipped as he rounded one end of the table. He grabbed the table runner to save himself, but that did no good. He fell on one knee, and the table runner carried with it vase, flowers and all, which came tumbling to the floor just in time to fall on Billy's head. It hurt him not at all, but really did him a good turn as it washed the sticky dough from his horns and eyes, for which he was truly thankful.

This little delay gave Mr. Robinson time to pick himself up and escape through the hall and up the front stairs, which he took two at a time. He rushed to his wife's room, expecting to find the door

93

Billy Whiskers at Home

unlocked, but alas, it was bolted and he heard his wife calling, "Help! Help! Burglars!" out of the window.

"Mary, Mary!" he shouted. "Let me in! Unbolt the door! It it I, your husband!"

But she was too frightened to recognize his voice, and would not leave the window through which she was leaning to call for help.

Now the door to her room had an extra large transom over it, plenty large enough for a person to climb through, and Mr. Robinson grabbed a stool in the hallway, pushed it under the transom and succeeded in raising himself up on the ledge of the door where he hung balancing himself on his stomach when he heard Billy come clattering up the stairs.

"Mary, Mary, open the door quickly! Stop that calling! Don't

Billy Whiskers at Home

you hear me? It is I, your husband!" he shouted at her again.

But his wife only saw a man climbing through her transom and thought it was one of the burglars she had heard downstairs, and leaned still further out of the window in an attempt to see someone coming along the street. She lost her balance and fell head first out of the window, but as luck would have it, she landed in a soft flower bed, and the window not being so very far from the ground, the fall did not injure her in the least.

At the moment she fell, Billy reached the head of the stairs. Seeing Mr. Robinson dangling there, half in and half out, he jumped on the stool and gave him a mighty butt that shoved him all the way through, and he landed on the floor of his wife's room all in a heap. In a moment he was on his feet and rushed to the window to see if his wife had been killed by her fall, forgetting all about Billy in his anxiety about his wife.

Billy's prey having thus escaped him, and hearing footsteps on the stairs, he knew somebody was answering Mrs. Robinson's cries for help. He ran down the long hall, hoping to find a back stairway, for he well knew if he was caught by the police or whoever it was coming to the rescue, they would club him. He was in luck, for he came to a pair of stairs leading straight down to an outside back porch. And in a jiffy he was out in the alley, running

95

for dear life, trying to put as much distance between himself and the Robinson house as he could.

All this time his tongue was half killing him with pain, and it was now so swollen he could not close his mouth. He was wild for a drink of water. He remembered he had seen a lovely sparkling fountain, and he was increasing his speed so he would reach it quickly when he heard a noise behind him that sounded like a patrol wagon coming lickety-split down the street. However, it proved to be just a truck full of men, and Billy thought, "I have no fear of *them*," when suddenly the truck stopped as it was about to pass him, and one of the men exclaimed, "There he is now! The very goat we are looking for!" and two fellows leaped out after him.

"Oh, no, you don't!" said Billy to himself, and he kicked up his heels and sped down the street and around the corner of the alley. The men ran after him as fast as ever they could and the truck followed but when they reached the corner, no goat was in sight.

"Drat that old rascal! He is hiding somewhere! But where I can't imagine as all I see are high back yard walls and fences, with not an open gate any place," said one of the men.

Just then three shrill screams rent the air about half way down the alley. The men knew immediately that Billy must have run into a yard and frightened some woman.

96

Billy Whiskers at Home

They were right in this surmise. Being a good jumper, Billy had leaped over a wall and landed in a beautiful garden where a hammock was swung between two trees. A lovely young lady lay in it, reading a book and eating fruit. On seeing a big, white goat leap over the fence and come straight towards her, she tried to get out of the hammock. But you know what a hammock is when you try to get out of one in a hurry? It simply turned upside down and she was in a heap on the grass, with fruit, pillows and book all about her, and she began to scream and call for help.

Billy grabbed a pear and trotted on through the yard. At that second a big touring car was backed out of the garage by a chauffeur, and being fond of riding in any kind of an automobile, Billy ran across the lawn and with one bound was in the tonneau. This so surprised the chauffeur that instead of stopping the car, he stepped on the accelerator and the car shot out to the street at forty miles an hour. The moment they were leaving in this manner, three men climbed over the back wall, one ran after the car and the goat and the other two went to the aid of the young woman who was still pleading for aid at the top of her voice. She had rolled around in trying to regain her feet so that instead of freeing herself, she had wound herself up in hammock and pillows until she was helpless. The men quickly had her on her feet and then they all ran to the front yard to discover what had become of the car and Billy.

97

Billy Whiskers at Home

Far down the street they could see a large crowd had gathered and they hurried along, sure it must be caused by a wreck of the car in which Billy rode.

"Wait until I tell our truck driver to come around on the street and pick us up," said one of the men as they ran. "We'll get there that way quicker than by foot."

What really had happened was this:

When the chauffeur came to his senses, he tried to slow down but he did not do so quickly enough and at a cross street he collided with a milk wagon, upsetting it and spilling out all the milk cans. The impact threw the chauffeur out of his car and stunned him for a minute. The truck carrying the men came up just then, they picked him up and put him in the truck, while one of them drove the auto back to the garage. No harm was done the car with the exception of scraping off a little paint, and, forgetting the loss of milk, the milk wagon suffered not at all. And now where was the cause of all this commotion, Mr. Billy Whiskers?

He was quietly drinking water from a crystal fountain in some private grounds, and I am glad to say that the swelling of his tongue was fast going down.

"Mercy! I believe I am tired! Guess I'll just go over under those bushes and take a nap," he thought.

This he did, but he slept much longer than he had intended, for

Billy Whiskers at Home

when he awoke the sun was going down, and he decided to try to find Ruthie once more. He had just stepped out into the street, when who should he see driving down his way but Mr. Watson with Ruthie on his lap. They had hunted and hunted for Billy with no success at all and had finally decided to go home without the goat, getting the cart some other day. They were as glad to see Billy as Billy was to see them. Mr. Watson stepped out of his buggy and tied Billy under it, then driving slowly, they went home to the farm.

Thus ended a very exciting day for Billy.

CHAPTER XII

THE TWINS ARE STOLEN

IN the forenoon of the next day Billy, Nannie, Daisy and Billy Junior were under the big elm tree in the barnyard listening to Billy describe all that had happened to him the day before while he was in town, when Stubby came running down the lane. On reaching them he panted out this message:

"Do you know where the Twins are while you are all chatting here?"

"I thought they were down by the stream playing," answered Daisy, their mother.

"No, they are being carried off to Milwaukee in a butcher's wagon!" announced Stubby.

"You don't mean it!" exclaimed Billy.

"How do you know?" asked Billy Junior, their father.

"Just saw them! I was running along the road, coming home from visiting the dogs over on the Samuelson farm when I heard the most pitiful crying as a wagon passed me. Stopping to listen, I recognized Judy's voice saying, 'I want to go home to my mama!

Billy Whiskers at Home

You're a naughty man to carry us off! If you don't let us out of this wagon, my grandpa will butt you when he catches you!'

" 'Yes, he will!' cried Punch. 'And my papa will help my grandpa butt and hook you! Stop and let us jump out!'

"It was while they were crying the wagon passed me, and I barked, 'Stop crying, Punch and Judy! I will bring your grandfather!'

" 'Oh, Uncle Stubby, do get us away from this naughty man! He is a butcher and we are afraid he will kill us. Oh, oh, oh! Do hurry and get us out of here before he makes us up into chops!'

"I trotted along behind the wagon and talked to them, telling them to cease crying or they would make themselves sick, and that I would go along with them and see what I could do.

"When we were passing the mill, who should come out but Button. He followed too, and I explained the situation to him and told him to stay with the Twins and find out where the butcher took them; that as soon as he knew this, he was to hurry back here and tell you; that if some one did not go along with them and tell us where they had been taken, we never could find them in a big city like Milwaukee. While he was doing that, I would return to the farm for you and then we would all go and rescue the Twins from the butcher. Picking them up on the road the way he did was nothing less than stealing."

"Come, let's not stop to talk another minute," said the Twins' father, as he kissed his wife good-by and told her not to cry, assuring he would bring their darlings back with him when he came.

"I know, Billy Junior, but it is a *butcher* who has them, and he will probably try to kill them to-night so that in case any one searches for them it will be impossible to find them, while if they were alive it would be comparatively easy to locate them."

"Oh, mother, isn't it awful to think of those darling babies being butchered? And they are all alone! I shall go crazy if they are not brought back," wailed Daisy to Nannie after Stubby, Billy and Billy Junior had departed.

"I know, my dear, just how you feel," answered Nannie, "but let us trust in God and wait. I feel sure Billy and their father will reach the Twins in time to rescue them. Probably while the butcher is eating his supper they will butt down the stable door and save them. Let us hope so, at any rate."

While Daisy and Nannie were trying to cheer one another, the two goats and Stubby were running like mad down the road towards Milwaukee. The sun was setting when they saw a big cloud of dust in the distance, and at last who should they discover to

Billy Whiskers at Home

be making it but Button! He had followed the butcher home and as soon as he had seen the Twins taken from the wagon and put in an open pen in the stable yard, he started back to tell the others where the Twins were. Button reported all this the moment they met on the road and he turned to hasten back to Mil-

waukee with them. When they arrived at the butcher's home, they were glad to see that his house was on the outskirts of the city and quite detached from those of his neighbors. It was now dark, but through the lighted window they could see the butcher eating his supper.

"Now is our time," said Billy. "I'll just butt down a rail in this fence and make a place large enough for us to crawl through. Then I will do the same thing with the pen where the Twins are imprisoned. We will have them out of here and on the way home in a jiffy. Billy Junior, you stand at the foot of the kitchen steps and if the butcher starts to come outdoors, butt him hard enough

Billy Whiskers at Home

to make him senseless so as to give us ample time to get away."

Just then a dog came bounding out of the barn, but he soon wished he had stayed where he was for in a moment Stubby and Button both were on him. His howl brought the butcher to the kitchen door. Seeing two dogs (he supposed Button was a dog) he grabbed a mop that stood beside the door and ran to the dog's rescue—but what was that which first struck him in the middle of the back and then chased him into the barn, where he received a butt that sent him up into the haymow?

The moment Billy Junior saw the butcher land in the hay, he gave the dog Stubby and Button were fighting a butt that sent him sky high, landing him on the roof of an outshed where he stood for a while too dazed to know what happened to him. Then Billy Junior hurried to help his father, but Billy Whiskers and the Twins had disappeared, so he knew they were already on the road toward home. Maybe you think those kids did not run fast when once they found themselves free!

As for the man who had stolen them, he was so bruised, he never even looked in the direction of the pen where he had put the kids. All he thought of was to get some liniment for his back. His poor dog stayed on the roof of the shed all night, much too frightened to attempt to get down.

When the Whiskers family was all together once again, Judy

105

Billy Whiskers at Home

said, "And what do you  think, mama, the old naughty butcher said as he leaned over the pen and looked at us before he went in for his supper? 'You are two pretty fine looking kids, and if I was not so tired and it was not so dark, I would butcher you to-night and sell your nice fat tender little chops in the morning. But I guess I will wait until it is light to-morrow and then kill you before anyone comes around looking for you. So ta-ta until then, my tender young kids!'"

"Yes," said Punch. "That is just what he said. He had the meanest face you ever saw. When I grow up I am going to go to Milwaukee and look for him, and butt him until he cries for mercy, so I am!"

"I wish you children to promise me now that you will never go out in the road alone again. Some member of your family must

Billy Whiskers at Home

always be with you, for you see now how easily you can be kidnaped. If Uncle Stubby had not just happened to be on the road, you would never have been rescued," said their mother.

"We promise! We promise! And cross our hearts we never will go in the road alone!"

CHAPTER XIII

TROUBLE OVER GINGER COOKIES

A FEW days after all this excitement Billy went over to Mr. Goodrich's farm, which was near that of Mr. Watson, to have a chat with the goats there. On his way to the pasture where the goats were grazing, he had to pass the kitchen door which happened to be open and through which came the delicious odor of hot ginger cookies.

"Yum, yum! How I do love ginger cookies," thought Billy. "I'll just take a peek, and see if I cannot get one."

Cautiously creeping up the kitchen steps, he peeped in. Seeing no one but spying a whole bread board covered with the cookies which had just been taken from the pans to cool, he skipped across the floor and rolled three or four into his mouth, when he heard some one coming up out of the cellar and he made his escape in a hurry. He had reached the bottom of the steps when he saw two little boys coming from the barnyard carrying a basket of eggs between them. He crept under the steps so they would not see him.

109

Billy Whiskers at Home

Within a few feet of the house, one stopped short, grabbed the other by the arm, exclaiming as he did so:

"Joe, I smell ginger cookies! Come, let's hurry and get Augusta to give us some. Oh, Augusta," raising his voice, "do give us some cookies! They smell too good for anything!"

"Yes, do, Gustie! I just *love* your cookies. They are so much better than our cook makes."

Good-natured Augusta was about to give them half a dozen or so when she noticed that some had already been taken.

"No, I won't give you any more. You have already helped your-selves to half a pan of them. Do you think I have nothing to do but make cookies for you two to eat like little pigs?"

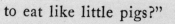

"What are you talking about, Gusta? We just this minute came in the door. We never touched your cookies!"

"Honestly we didn't," said Joe, backing up Ned.

"You needn't

add lying to your stealing! Guess I know! Those cookies go just twelve in a pan, and four of them are gone. Do you mean to tell me they put on their hats and went out for a walk? Shame on you, boys, for lying to me!"

"But I tell you, Gusta, we never touched them or as much as knew they were here until we came in the door. You came in the same moment we did. And here we are standing over on this side of the room and the cookies are away over there on that side. Now tell me how we could have gotten them."

"Well, you may have been over here and grabbed them and run back to the door when you heard me coming," she said slowly.

"But we didn't, and you are a mean old thing to accuse us of lying and stealing—two things we do not do!"

"Oh, merciful goodness!" exclaimed Augusta, throwing up her hands and looking with horror at her clean kitchen floor. "See, see! Some one has been in here and tracked mud all over my floor!"

"Ha, ha! See there, now! Whoever did that stole your cookies too," said Joe.

"I bet it was the grocery boy, as no one else comes around here," said Augusta.

"Gusta, you are too quick to accuse people when you really have no reason to do so. These are not the footprints of a person at all but of some animal, and the tracks look like those of a sheep or a goat."

"So they do! Well, just wait until I find the animal and I will give it a good beating with my broom," she threatened. "I don't care so much for the cookies as I do about the floor, for now I shall have to scrub it again, and there is no fun in getting down on my rheumatic knees to clean this floor."

While Augusta was grumbling, the boys edged their way over to the table and helped themselves to three cookies apiece.

"Oh, Gusta, quick! I smell something burning," cried Ned. "It must be more cookies."

Horrors! When she reached the oven door and opened it, a cloud of black smoke rushed out and when she carried her pan of cookies over to the table she saw at a glance they were burned to a crisp.

"Here, Ned, take them out and throw them in the swill pail," she said.

This the boy did, and presently Augusta, Ned and Joe had the pleasure of seeing a big white goat dancing around like mad. Billy had gone to the pail to eat the discarded cookies, and not knowing they were so hot, had taken two, one of which stuck to the roof of his mouth, burning him dreadfully and causing him to dance with the pain.

Billy Whiskers at Home

"There is your cookie thief, Gusta! You better go after him with your broom," said Ned.

Augusta grabbed the broom and rushed toward Billy, but Billy was in no mood to be reproved in this manner, so when she was near him he surprised her by butting her right over his head, and she landed in the horse's drinking trough with a great splash. The boys, enjoying all this, began to throw the eggs from their basket at Billy. Of course when they hit him they broke and the yellow yolks ran all over his nice white coat. This angered him and he ran toward the house to butt the boys, but they leaped inside the door and shut it, throwing more eggs at him from the safety of the window.

Just now Mrs. Goodrich entered the kitchen and seeing the boys throwing eggs from the basket, exclaimed, "Boys, boys! What are you doing? What do you mean by throwing nice fresh eggs at something?"

"Oh, we forgot they were *eggs!* We were throwing them at a big, cross white goat outside. He has just butted Gusta into the watering trough, and we were trying to chase him away. Here he comes up the steps now!"

Bing, bing, bangety-bing! Two hard butts in quick succession on the kitchen door. As it was not tightly closed, it flew open and in came Billy, looking for his tormentors. One dove under the table, the other stepped up on the table right on top of the cookies, while

113

Billy Whiskers at Home

Mrs. Goodrich plunged into the dining room and barricaded the door by pushing the dining table against it and piling the chairs on top of it.

Billy tried to get at the boy under the table but could not do so as the table stood against the wall. But he could reach the boy on top of the table by climbing on a chair beside it. This he did but as he came up one side, the boy jumped down the other, upset the table and the beloved cookies rolled in all directions. Seeing this, Billy let the boys escape and turned his attention to eating every cookie he could find. He had just concluded he had found them all, even to the one he pawed out from under the stove when who should appear in the doorway but the hired man, pitchfork in hand. He was evidently in pursuit of Billy Whiskers. Now there was one thing Billy feared and that was a pitchfork.

Billy Whiskers at Home

He had good reason to do so, for he had been chased with them and had had them stuck in his sides many, many times. Consequently on seeing this man standing in the doorway armed with one, he looked around for a way to get out of the room. There was the door into the dining room so well barricaded by Mrs. Goodrich and the outside door guarded by the man with the pitchfork. Oh, *there* was a flight of stairs and without a moment's hesitation he ran up them, the man close behind, trying his best to reach him with the long-handled fork. Arriving at the top, he saw another flight leading down into the front hall. Down these he plunged, but half way down he encountered Mrs. Goodrich. She was so frightened at seeing the big goat coming toward her that she lost her balance and went rolling to the bottom. Billy ran into the living room and thank goodness, a window was open. He jumped through and made his escape down the road. By the time the hired man had picked up Mrs. Goodrich and had satisfied himself no bones were broken, Billy was out of sight and there was no telling in which direction he had gone. So he went around to the kitchen to see how Augusta was getting along. He found her all right physically but mentally she was mad as a wet cat. For had not Olie, her best beau, seen her in a very undignified position, sitting in the watering trough with legs hanging over and struggling to get out? And worse yet, he had laughed when he tried to help her out. He could not control himself for she looked too funny stuck fast in the trough. And so now all she would say was:

"Olie Oleson, I will never, no, *never* speak another word to you as long as I live! So *there!*"

Olie had heard this threat many times before so that it did not bother him in the least, for he knew the very next time she saw him she would have forgotten all about her threat.

"I believe I won't go back and see the goats this morning but wait until these people cool off," thought Billy. "If that hired man should happen to see me down in the pasture, he might take a shot at me. My, but those ginger cookies were good! Wish I could have taken some to Nannie and the rest of the family at home. The Twins especially would have been delighted with them. I don't see why goats and animals don't have pockets in the sides of their skins. It would be such a convenience for them to be able to take presents home to their families and to carry a lunch sometimes when they have no idea when they will be able to find food the next time."

And so musing, Billy went home.

CHAPTER XIV

THE CHUMS HAVE A DAY OFF

O, Stubby and Button, come over here a minute!"

"All right," answered Button. "I'll be there as soon as I finish eating this fish head."

"How in the world can you enjoy those nasty, smelly things?"

"Why, they are delicious! Don't you know the old saying, 'The nearer the bone, the sweeter the meat'? Well, as these fish heads are all bone, that makes what little meat there is on them mighty sweet and toothsome."

"Oh, you are a regular epicure, you are!" exclaimed Billy.

"What do you want of us?" asked Stubby, coming up to Billy Whiskers.

"It is this: what do you say to our going into town and spending a day? It is so quiet out here where nothing ever happens that I feel I shall explode unless I hear a little noise and see something going on with a little life in it."

117

Billy Whiskers at Home

"Just the thing! Life out here is beginning to grow a little monotonous for me also after our exciting life of moving from one place to another almost every day."

"Oh, Button, leave your smelly old fish head and come here! Billy has a dandy plan for us all," called Stubby.

"Coming!" called the black cat. "I have just finished."

"No need for you to come here. We will pass you on the way we are going to take," said Billy.

"So you are going some place, are you? I was just thinking this morning that it was about time you were suggesting a trip somewhere, as you have remained here quite a while for you. And every so often the wanderlust strikes you and off you go. The only thing that would keep you here longer would be that you have been everywhere but to the North Pole and the South Pole. Each day I have been expecting you to propose a trip to the moon in an airship of some kind."

"No, I am not weary of the farm yet, but I feel I should like a little excitement just for a day to give a little spice to life."

"Well, what is the plan you have in mind?"

"Nothing much, only for us three to go into town and spend the day and return at nightfall."

"As wild as that, is it? Very well, I am with you for that trip.

Billy Whiskers at Home

But no more long trips, gallivanting all over the face of the globe for me for a year at least. I am tired seeing strange countries and foreign peoples for a while. I want to stay home and enjoy its quiet and comfort."

"Ho, you must be feeling old, Button, to speak like that. You, the friskiest cat in the world, talking of settling down!"

Half an hour later the three Chums were trotting down the alley back of the main street in town. They were about to pass a movie theater when, hearing the music and seeing the rear doors open for ventilation, they thought they would go in and have a peep at the film being run off.

Button being black as ink ran down the middle aisle without being seen, but just then three or four people stepped into the aisle to go out and Button dodged under a lady's seat. She did not see the cat but felt something soft rub across her legs. Immediately she thought it was a big rat and gave one blood-curdling scream that upset the entire audience for they did not know what had happened, and all rushed frantically from the theater. All because one unseen cat had rubbed against a woman!

The proprietor rushed out on the stage in front of the curtain to discover the cause of the panic but all he saw were empty seats and the crowd pushing and hurrying pell-mell out the doors. As he stood there trying to fathom the trouble, he saw in the darkness among the empty seats two bright yellow lights flash from aisle to aisle under the seats and then over them.

"Great Scott! What can that be? Whatever it is, it must be what frightened the people away. Ikey, come here quick, and tell me what it is I see!"

"Are you crazy? Can't you tell what you see with your own eyes?" the boy asked.

"Look over in that dark corner, and tell me if you see two yellow balls of fire jumping here and there and everywhere."

"Yes, I do. And I see nothing but just those two spots. What is more, I am going to get out, for now they are coming straight this way!"

Both man and boy hurried behind the screen and were beginning to tell the people working about the theater what they had seen when cool as you please out walked Button from behind the screen and stood gazing at them.

"Holy Moses, those lights we saw were only the yellow eyes of this cat! But look, Ikey, he is black all over. A black cat has walked across our stage. That means bad luck for us."

"No, it doesn't, you superstitious old man! Black cats or white cats can't bring or take good luck or bad. In this age we don't believe in such things."

Billy Whiskers at Home

"Anyhow get him out of here! Get him out of here! For he has driven all our audience away."

"Well, what do you care, Solomon? They have paid their money. What does it matter whether or not they see the picture? Their money is all you want. But I'll drive him out for you anyway," and a book was hurled at Button's head by a man standing by an open window a few feet away from the cat.

Button dodged the book, then with a long leap went flying over the man's head and through the open window out into the alley, where by chance he happened to alight on the back of a passing dog. Feeling Button's claws dig into him, he set up a howl and ran down the alley lickety-split. He passed Billy and Stubby, who stood aside and laughed so heartily at the sight of Button clinging to the dog's back that they nearly fell over in their merriment. But even as they looked, the dog ducked down and crawled under a fence, scraping Button off. Billy and Stubby ran down the alley where Button stood, too dazed and bruised to move for he had received a hard bump on his head when the dog crawled under the fence.

"For pity's sake, how did you happen to be playing circus with that dog?" asked Billy.

"If you could only have seen yourself, you would have died with laughter. You looked so comical all hunched up riding on that dog's back."

"And so would you have been hunched up if you had been trying to stick on, not by the skin of your teeth but by your claws which kept slipping. I knew if I let go I should have a terrible tumble."

"Here come the people out of the back of that theater, looking for you. We better be going," said Billy. And so the three trotted down the alley until they came to a cross street. They had gone but a little way down this street when they came to a grocery store.

"I think I shall leave you fellows here and go on and see if I cannot find something to eat to my liking," said Stubby. "Where shall we meet when it is time to go home, and at what time shall we meet?"

"At the crossroads at the edge of town, around six o'clock," replied Billy. "What are you two going to do?"

"Oh, I don't know. Just walk along and see what turns up," said Stubby.

"And you, Button?"

"Tag along with you, Billy, until I think of something I should like to do."

Billy Whiskers at Home

"So long then, until we meet again!"

Stubby ran through the side door of the grocery and found himself in a kind of store room and shipping room combined, as there were shelves full of canned goods, boxes of crackers and breakfast foods, while on the floor were baskets of groceries ready to be delivered. All around the room next to the wall were ranged barrels of molasses, kerosene, vinegar and such things.

Just as Stubby entered, a boy came in to get a box of crackers from a high shelf and as he reached for it his foot slipped and in trying to save himself from falling, the box dropped out of his hands and went crashing to the floor, knocking off the lid and all the crackers spilling over the floor.

"Oh, see what I have done," he grumbled. "Spilled all those crackers, and spoiled them too, for after being on the dirty floor they will have to be thrown away."

At this moment he was called to the front of the store and the moment he left, Stubby came from behind the barrel where he had been hiding and ate the crackers. He ate every one and even licked up the crumbs, they were such good, fresh, crisp crackers. When the boy came back and saw they had disappeared he took it for granted that some one had swept them up. This time he had come for some molasses and while it was running into the quart measure, he took a handful of crackers and stuck them one by one under the molasses spigot, letting the molasses trickle all over them, and then putting the whole cracker in his mouth at once.

"Gee, but they do taste good! Almost as good as molasses candy!" he was saying when some one called him and he seized the quart measure and hurried away, forgetting to turn off the spigot.

Stubby had been watching all this and now ran over to the molasses barrel and let some of the sweet stuff drop into his mouth.

"My, oh my, that is almost as good as candy, just as the boy said! If I only had a cracker or two, I would be fixed. Why, there is the box now! I'll just go over and get a mouthful of crackers and bring them back and hold them under the spigot until they are covered with molasses, the way the boy did, and eat them whole."

All this time the molasses was running out on the floor, making a big puddle.

"Yum, yum! These crackers and molasses taste good! I just love molasses candy, and this is next thing to it. I must have another mouthful before some one comes and cleans up this mess," but he had not the time for just then the owner of the grocery entered the side door and seeing a stray dog in his store raised his leg to kick him out. But alas, as he lifted his foot, the other slipped in the molasses and he sat down squarely in it all.

"Who left that spigot turned on?" he roared.

Stubby waited to hear no more for he knew the poor boy would

Billy Whiskers at Home

be punished.   Not wishing to pass the man, and there being no other way out, Stubby decided to jump up on a high box and from it take a flying leap over the man's head out into the alley.   This he did and landed safely.   In a minute more there was no sight of a little stubby-tailed dog in that alley.

While Stubby was in the grocery store, Billy had wandered on a block or two when he heard a great hullabaloo in a back yard.

"I wonder what is going on there.   I'll just run along and peek in," he thought.

Arrived at the yard where he heard all the whistling and laughter, he peeked through the half open gate and this is what he saw: four boys trying to hitch a big dog to a little express wagon.   And they were having a most difficult time doing it for the dog would not stand up but insisted on crouching on the ground.   Two boys tried to hold him up while the other two adjusted the harness.   But no use; he would not stand up.   At last the boys grew provoked and the boy on either side of him gave the dog a cruel blow with a whip and pushed him forward.   In his surprise, the dog bounded forward. Once he was started the boys had no way of controlling him for the reins were dangling over his back.   His starting had surprised the boys as much as their whipping had surprised the dog.   Down the long back yard he went, dragging the little express wagon straight toward the gate through which Billy was peeping.   When he dashed

125

through it, the wheels on one side of the wagon collided with the gate post. This broke the traces, releasing the dog. Down the street he went like mad to escape his tormentors.

On reaching the gate the boys spied Billy. One lad, who had once owned a pair of goats and a little wagon, called out, "Come ahead, fellows! Let's hitch up the goat! He is a big, fine creature and can pull the wagon easier than the dog."

Almost before Billy knew what was happening, he found himself hitched to the little express wagon and being driven down the street. At first he enjoyed it, until too many boys got in the wagon at one time. This treatment made Billy angry and he decided to upset them the first opportunity he had. When he came to a place where the sidewalk was high from the street pavement, he ran off the walk, turning the little wagon completely upside down and spilling out all the boys. As Billy ran off, one boy caught hold of the reins that were dragging on the ground, jumped in the wagon which had righted itself by this time, and on down the street they went. When they came to a small bridge that spanned a wide ditch, Billy said to himself, "Here is where I lose the last boy!" and with extra exertion he ran faster than he had ever run in all his life. As he reached the bridge, instead of going over it he swerved and plunged down the bank right into the little stream which was narrow but deep. Here he spilled the boy out and while he was picking himself up, Billy

Billy Whiskers at Home

climbed up the opposite bank and headed for the crossroads where he had agreed to meet Stubby and Button.

He reached this rendezvous about ten minutes before the others. When they came and saw him standing in the traces half asleep, they wanted to know where and how he had acquired the wagon. He told them and added that he was going to take it home with him, and the boys could find it as best they could.

When the Chums reached the farm, Mr. Watson was sitting on his front porch reading, but he glanced up at the sound of wheels turning into his driveway and he had to laugh for there was Billy pulling a very new looking little express wagon, with Stubby and

Billy Whiskers at Home

Button sitting on the front seat. Indeed they had the appearance of driving the little turnout.

"Well, well, well! I wonder how Billy came by that wagon. Probably some little boy has hitched him to it and then hit him with a whip or done something to him he did not like and he has run off with the wagon. I expect in a short time some one will appear looking for it. In the meantime I will unhitch Billy and take care of the wagon."

But it was not until the next morning that any one came for it, as it took the boys all that time to discover where Billy had gone.

"SAVE ME QUICKLY, OR IT WILL BE TOO LATE!" GOBBLED THE TURKEY.
PAGE 154)

CHAPTER XV

BUTTING MATCHES

SHEP, the Watson dog, noticed that all the animals seemed greatly excited. They wandered around the farmyard, lay down for a few minutes and then got up up to begin their restless wandering again.

"Something is up, and I bet it is some devilment of Billy Whiskers. I'll just keep my eye on the villain without his knowing it and discover what it is that is going on," thought Shep.

Now the night pasture where the cows were allowed to wander after they had been milked in the evening was directly the other side of the barn. The gate between was left standing open so the cattle could pass from barnyard to pasture and back again at their pleasure. This pasture led down a steep hill to the stream and a nice grassy meadow, and as the banks of the stream were sandy, the cattle liked to go there to roll in the sand and dry their coats after a bath in the pools of the stream.

It was bright moonlight—one of those nights when the moon rose early. For which Shep was thankful, as it made it easy to watch the cattle. Just as he surmised, the minute the moon appeared over the top of the high hill in front of the house and shed its light over the barnyard and pasture, Billy Whiskers, Billy Junior, Nannie and Daisy slipped off the watch tower, as they called the high straw stack on which they slept, and from which vantage point they could see all that went on. They made straight for the pasture. Shep kept an eye on Billy, saw him lead his family through the gate into the pasture, and was a little amazed to find all the cattle followed them in groups of two and three.

"Now what in the world are they up to? I'll go up on the straw stack they just left and see where they go. Not one of them is stopping to take so much as a mouthful of clover, and that is really fine clover in their field, and generally they love to munch it when the dew is on it as now. So there must be something very exciting ahead of them. Now they are going down the hill toward the stream. What is that line of black I see coming from the Smith farm? I declare it is his cattle, even to the big hogs! There comes another line of cattle from the direction of the Jones farm. It must be a big party they are having."

When all the animals arrived at the edge of the stream where stretched the wide beach of sand, Shep could see they were forming a great circle.

Billy Whiskers at Home

"What is up, I wonder?" he said over and over to himself. But he did not have to wait long to know, for Billy stepped into the center of the ring and then out stepped Satan, one of the neighbor's big, coal-black goats, and joined him. After sniffing each other's noses, they backed off a few paces and then rushed toward one another with great force. There was a clash of horns, followed with a twisting of necks and much side-stepping until Billy had Satan down on his knees. After this they separated, each seeking his own particular

group of animal friends. In less time than it takes to tell, they were back in the middle of the ring fighting again. But they did not seem to be fighting to hurt one another, but rather to see which could butt the harder and down the other. They would advance slowly step by step, eyes unwinkingly on the adversary until within a few feet of touching noses. Then without a sound one or the other would spring forward and they would butt their foreheads together or lock horns. The way they would twist their necks one would certainly think they would break them. At other times they would stand on

131

their hind legs and push one another forward and backward, striking out with their fore legs.

All this time the onlookers pawed the ground in excitement and bellowed their pleasure or disgruntlement as their favorite was winning or losing.

Billy won the first round, and all the animals clustered around the contestants, complimenting them on their prowess and skill.

After Billy Whiskers and Satan had taken a drink and waded in the stream to cool off, they lay down to watch the next feature on the program. This was a test of strength between two blooded bulls, one a red Hereford, the other a red and white Durham. The Hereford was ever on the alert but much lighter in weight than the Durham, who was of powerful build. But even though he could hit the most powerful blow, the alert Hereford was likely to fly around and give him a couple punches in the ribs while he was slowly getting in position to hook him. It had been agreed they were not to run their horns into one another, as this was purely a friendly bout, just to exhibit their skill, and indeed it did prove to be a most exciting display of strength and quickness. They whirled and turned, locked horns and twisted each other's necks until one could almost hear the bones crack. Whenever they locked horns and it came to a display of strength, the Durham was away ahead, and he would push the Hereford into the stream, but when it came to hooking, as they would have done in a real fight, the Hereford was superior, for his long, sharp horns would have made short work of the big, clumsy Durham.

Next in order was a fight between two fat rams with double twisted horns, who fought standing facing each other, their big twisted horns locked together. They forced each other forward and backward across the ring, kicking up the dirt at a great rate. When time was called, it was found they could not unlock their horns. In fact, in the morning when Mr. Watson found them that way it took both him and his hired man quite a while to separate them.

This fight ended the evening's performance, which all had enjoyed so much that they planned then and there to have a second one a week from that night, which was to be for just the younger animals— the calves, colts, lambs and kids. Of course the Twins were the first to ask to be in it, and their parents saying they could, Billy Whiskers promised to give them some lessons to prepare them for the event.

Just before they separated, some one proposed they have an exhibition of jumping and running as well. This was considered a good proposal and was accepted unanimously, though every one said they knew just who would win those races: Sal Scrugs. She was known to be the highest jumper and fleetest runner of all the animals far and near.

Billy Whiskers at Home

"No, there is Shep," argued some one. "We must ask him to compete with her."

Some declared he would say no, while others were sure he would enjoy it. So it was left to Billy to approach him on the subject, and with many complimentary expressions for those who had participated, the animals separated, promising to be on hand at the next meeting.

CHAPTER XVI

THE DUCKS GROW DIZZY-HEADED

HE day after the butting match a laughable thing happened at the farm.

A big tub of cider was down in the orchard waiting for the kegs to put it in when some ducks on their way for a swim in the pond smelt something like rotten apples, a food all ducks like very much. They decided to stop and eat some. Consequently they flew up on the edge of the tub, and seeing it filled almost to overflowing, they thought it would be nice to go swimming in anything that smelt so good. Three old mother ducks and five young ones jumped in that cider. They tasted it and it was so refeshing a draught that they kept drinking as they swam about. The more they tasted it, the more they wanted. But presently they could not tell when they were drinking it and when they were not, as they felt queer in the head. Everything seemed to be running around like mad; even the wheelbarrows were going around

135

in circles with no person pushing them, while the big barn was swaying as in a gale.

At last one old duck quacked to another, "Sister, just see how crazily everything in the barnyard is acting. Even the barn itself looks as if it would topple over."

"It certainly does! I was noticing it when you spoke," said a second.

"We better go over and see what causes it," suggested the third old duck.

The young ducks, on being asked, preferred to stay where they were and swim around.

"My, what is the matter with this tub? It doesn't stand still, and I cannot get out. It is acting just the same as everything over in the barnyard!"

"It must be we are having some kind of a storm. Perhaps it is a radio storm. Not that I ever heard of a radio storm, but I will wager there *are* such things. There are so many new things these days, one can't say there can't be such a thing, for if they do, there it is the next day right before them."

"Well, I declare," exclaimed one old duck as she fell over on her side, "this tub rocks so it made me tumble over, and to save my life I can't get back on the right rim of this tub. There are two rims

Billy Whiskers at Home

and every time I step on one it is not there.   What can be the matter? My head feels so dizzy.   Does yours?"

"I should think it did!   And my ears ring something dreadful!"

"There it is again!   To save my life I can't sit up straight with this tub running around in circles as it does."

"We better make an extra effort to get out of this tub, for it might be possible that this yellow fluid has affected us."

"Now you have found the trouble!   The stuff we have been drinking is the cause of our dizziness, I am sure of it."

Just then Shep and the hired man came along the path.   Seeing the ducks in the tub, Shep tried to frighten them, but they only quacked and then left their bills stretched open, too crazy-headed to shut them.   The more Shep barked at them, the more they quacked and flapped their wings, but they could not get out of the tub.   When the hired man reached them, he nearly died laughing at the queer actions of the ducks. He picked them up one after the other and set them on the ground, but then they only made him laugh the more for they stepped so

Billy Whiskers at Home

high and waddled along with such a rolling gait, their heads held to one side in such a peculiar manner, he doubled up with mirth.

But this was not all of it. He turned over the tub of cider—there was nothing else to do after the ducks had been in it. But little did he think what a commotion it was going to create among the fowls. When the geese came along on their way to the pond and smelled the cider and saw it running on the ground in little rivulets, they craned their long necks to get a better smell. This second whiff only assured them the liquid was surely made of apples. They began to drink all they could catch in their bills as it ran along the hard-beaten path. Soon they too were lifting their feet so high that their big bodies toppled over and at last they just rolled on the grass, their legs sticking straight up in the air, where they lay hissing until the hired man came and carried them off to the goose house. Before night even the turkeys and chickens had had some of the troublesome cider. In consequence the old turkey gobbler nearly gobbled his head off as he puffed himself out and went strutting uncertainly about the yard. As for the roosters, they crowed and crowed and crowed until they fell off the fence from sheer exhaustion. Really it was as comical a sight as any one could well imagine to see the fowls reeling and staggering around the barnyard in such a ridiculous manner.

Mr. Watson had several orders for geese, ducks and chickens to be filled the next morning. He generally had a difficult time catching just the ones he wished to sell, but for a wonder to-night he could walk right up to any fowl and pick it up without it so much as lifting a wing in flight or making a single outcry. You see the cider had made them so stupid they were nearly sound asleep.

CHAPTER XVII

THE NEW ELECTRIC WASHER

NY one who has ever lived in the country and kept turkeys and peacocks knows the moment a stranger drives by, those fowls give the alarm as surely as a good watchdog barks, only they set up a terrible clatter, the peacock by jumping on something high and screeching out his discordant call that carries a long way, it is so penetrating, and old Mr. Turkey Gobbler spreading his tail and wings so wide they drag on the ground as he puffs himself out with pride until he looks as if he would surely burst.

Consequently when Hiram, the hired man on the Watson farm, heard the racket in the barnyard, he walked to the door to see who was coming. There turning in the drive was a delivery wagon bringing the new electric washing machine Mr. Watson had bought. Hiram put down his pitchfork and went to help the men unload it and set it up. Of course, Billy Whiskers, that old Curiosity Shop, had to go too, for it would never do to have anything new come to

Billy Whiskers at Home

the farm and Billy not know about it. Neither would it do to have Billy do or see anything Stubby and Button missed. And of course when the Twins saw their grandfather and their Uncle Stubby and Uncle Button going any place, they had to go along. So when Hiram thought he heard footsteps behind him and turned his head to look, what should he see but quite a procession tagging behind him.

"Well, I declare to goodness if that old Billy isn't the most curious animal I ever ran across! He tags me from morning until night, so I almost feel I had a tail tied to me!"

"Oh, Hiram!" called Mr. Watson, "come and help us put up the washing machine!"

"Coming! Coming!" answered Hiram.

After an hour of pulling, hauling and lifting, with every one bossing every one else and stepping on one another's fingers and toes, to say nothing of Billy Whiskers adding to the confusion by being under their feet, the necessary electric wiring was completed and the washing machine was in place.

Billy Whiskers at Home

Button had climbed on top of a cupboard in the laundry, thinking this would be a fine place from which to see all that went on and still escape being kicked or put out. Stubby had run under the table and jumped into a clothes basket where he would be out of the way and still could watch every move made. As for Billy, he was here, there and everywhere, under every one's feet and running across their paths and getting in the way generally, being put out of the laundry one minute and returning the next when they were busy over the machine.

At last it was set up and ready to start, and the man who had brought it from town walked over to the wall and touched a black button. The water began to churn round and round a piece of clothing the man had put in the washer to show them how quickly it would be washed clean.

Billy was so interested that he walked straight up to it and stuck his nose against the glass case, for what puzzled him most was how the water got in the tub when he had seen no one pour it in, and he knew the water nearest at hand was away down in the pond at the foot of the hill.

As for Button, he stretched his neck so far over the top of the cupboard that he nearly toppled off, and Stubby barked in his surprise and kept jumping in and out of the basket. In fact, he was so nervous he did not know what he was doing.

Billy Whiskers at Home

Swish! Swish! Swish! went the water, becoming all foamy and white.

As Button gazed, the machine stopped and the water grew still. Then all of a sudden it began to swish around again, though no person was near it. The person nearest the machine was a man standing by the wall, his finger on a little black button in the wall, while next him stood Hilda, clapping her hands in delight. You see, she did the washing.

"Now it will be only child's play to do the washing, even though we do have big tablecloths and sheets," she said.

They were all leaving the laundry and Billy was about to go too, when he found himself all tangled up with the tube that let the water into the tub and the electric wires that furnished the power to run the machine. The first thing he knew he felt prickles running all over him, and then a queer, jerky feeling as if some one were pulling all the muscles in his body the wrong way,—and that is the last he knew for a long time. Billy had suffered a shock that knocked him over and made him unconscious!

MR. WATSON'S HIRED MAN SOON HAD A ROPE AROUND BILLY'S NECK.
(PAGE 168)

Billy Whiskers at Home

When Mr. Watson turned to see why Billy did not come, and discovered him stretched on the floor as if dead, he knew not what to think until he saw the detached wires. Then he knew Billy had suffered a shock of electricity. The men jumped off the wagon and with the help they gave, Mr. Watson and Hiram soon had Billy all right once more.

"Mr. Watson, you need not worry. He is not killed for the current in these machines is not strong enough to hurt any one, much less kill them," said one of the men.

That very evening when Billy, his family, Stubby and Button and a few friends were resting by the straw stack, they wished to hear from Billy's own lips how a shock of electricity felt. He told them: "You haven't any idea what a peculiar sensation it is. At first I felt all prickly, as if some one was sticking me full of needles and pins. Then all my muscles began to double up, and that is the last I knew about until I found myself on the grass outside the laundry with Mr. Watson and the men working over me. Not a pleasant sensation at all. I hope, I assure you, that Hilda never has one. It would almost kill her if she did."

Just before luncheon that day Stubby and Button had had a very exciting experience. They had been coming home from Mr. Jones' farm when they heard a child crying. They looked everywhere, but still they could not see any child, and when they tried to follow the sound, it first led them in one direction and then in another.

Presently Stubby said, "It seems to me the cry comes from the stone quarry. Let's go and look."

So the two ran up the steep side of the quarry and looked down into the deep pit half-filled with water. At first they saw nothing. Then they thought they distinguished something white floating on the water close to the opposite side of the pit.

"Look, Button! You have sharper eyes than I. What do you make out that white thing to be over there?"

"Heavens! It is a child's face. Did you ever see anything so white in all your life?"

At that moment the child saw Stubby and Button, and began to cry anew.

"Do you hear, Button? From the sound of that cry the child is almost exhausted from calling for help and from fright at being in the water."

"I should think it would be. What are we to do to get it out? It is a little boy. I know by his coat, for he raised his arms to signal to us."

"Here comes a farmer. Let us run down and bark just as he is opposite the quarry. I'll bark and you meow and we will run in front of his horse and make such a fuss he will know there must be something the matter in the quarry pit and perhaps he will stop and go to see. Let's hope so, at any rate."

The minute they disappeared, the child began to cry more pitifully than ever, for of course he thought they had run away and left him to his fate.

Nearer and nearer came the old rattling wagon, the driver whistling as hard as ever he could.

"You see," said Stubby, "his wagon is making such a rumble he would never have heard the child crying."

"He is almost here. Now let us start," said Button.

Down the steep side of the quarry they plunged pellmell, and jumped out before the horses so suddenly they leaped to one side of the road and stopped short. It was done so quickly it nearly threw the man off the seat.

"Say, Stub and Button, what did you do that fool thing for?"

You see the man knew the two very well, for he was Mr. Watson's hired man.

"You nearly scared the life out of the horses and came near upsetting me in the bargain. Well, well, will you look at those fool animals chasing each other up the steep side of the quarry? Here they come down again! And they stand and look at me as if they were trying to tell me something. Heigho, if they aren't going up again and looking down into the pit and barking and meowing like

147

Billy Whiskers at Home

mad. Hark! Did I hear a child cry?" He put his hand to his ear and turned his head in that direction. Sure enough, the cry was repeated. "Jehoshaphat, I bet a child has fallen into the quarry and that is  what those smart animals are trying to let me know about."

With one bound he was out of the wagon and climbing up the side of the quarry as fast as he could go, loose stones and dirt flying in a shower behind him as he was in such a hurry to reach the top. The second he got there, he discovered the pale face of the child as it showed so plainly against the wet, black stones. He ran around the pit until he was directly over where the child lay.

"Uncle Hiram, come quick! Come quick! I can't hang on much longer. My fingers are getting numb!"

You see the man was no other than the little child's own Uncle.

 Down the steep side of the quarry he started, but found he must go further along the top and then down, as the stones were soft and broke under his feet and he feared they might injure the child as they rolled.

148

Billy Whiskers at Home

When the little fellow saw the man start to go down to him again he cried out in fright and dismay: "Oh, Uncle Hiram, don't! Don't go away and leave me!"

"Don't worry, Eddie. Indeed I won't leave you. I am just going over here a little way to find a better and safer place to climb down."

In fact, he was soon down and walking along a rocky ledge that led straight to where the little fellow lay, and in a jiffy he had him in his arms and was climbing the steep ascent, the child clasped in a close embrace. When they were safely on the wagon, he asked the boy how he happened to fall in the pit and he said he was coming home from doing an errand and was walking near the edge of the quarry when he saw a beautiful blue flower on the very edge and while trying to get it the bank gave way and fell into the water in the quarry pit, carrying him down with it.

"How long had you been there?"

"Oh, ever and ever so long, Uncle! Seemed most like a year!"

"I'll wager it does seem like a year and more to you, and I never would have found you if it had not been for Stubby and Button. The old wagon was making such a racket and I was whistling so loudly I never would have heard you cry above all that noise."

Looking down the road he saw a woman who seemed much excited running in their direction and when they drew near enough to distinguish who it was, they found it was Eddie's mother, looking for him. He had not come back from the errand on which she had sent him, telling him to hurry home. As he was an obedient son, she feared some ill had befallen him and was searching for him. How she cried for joy when she had him in her arms and knew he was safe! She declared she wanted to see Stubby and Button and pet them and give them the biggest chicken dinner they had ever had to show her appreciation.

"They are such smart animals, I know they will understand everything you say to them, and enjoy and thank you for the dinner," said Mr. Watson's hired man. "I'll bring them over with me to-morrow when I pass your house on my way to the mill."

Thus another good deed was added to the long list of those done by Stubby and Button as the years went by.

CHAPTER XVIII

CATCHING THE THANKSGIVING TURKEY

IT was the night before Thanksgiving rather than Christmas, and in the house all was quiet as a mouse. But not so in the barnyard. Everything there was confusion and hubbub for the biggest, fattest turkey gobbler of the flock was to be captured and killed for the Thanksgiving feast. He had lived to see all his flock slain with the exception of a young gobbler and three or four turkey hens. Consequently when he saw a boy and a man come into the barnyard and walk toward him, holding out hands filled with corn and wheat, he had his suspicions. He had seen sixty or seventy members of his flock go up to men to eat from their hands only to be grabbed by the neck and carried off, never to be seen again. It was because of this that when any one offered him anything to eat, no matter what it was, he drew in his feathers, stuck out his neck and ran for dear life and hid until they had left the barnyard.

It was growing dusk now and he had just fallen into a doze as he rested in his usual roosting place on the lower limb of an old oak tree behind the woodpile. Suddenly he was rudely awakened by some one catching hold of one of his legs. He roused with a start to find it was a big boy trying to capture him. With a spasm of fear he flapped his wings and tried to fly to a higher limb, but he was unable to do that for the boy grasped one of his legs firmly and pulled him back.

Just then the gobbler spied Billy Whiskers standing by the wood-pile and he gobbled for him to aid him. "Save me! Save me, Billy!"

In a flash Billy ran up the woodpile on which the boy was stand-ing. This started the wood to rolling, and the boy was forced to release the turkey's leg or have his own broken in a fall.

"Oh, Billy, why *can't* you mind your own business and not stick your nose into what doesn't concern you?" he exclaimed.

The moment the old gobbler was released, he tried to decide which would be the safer place for him; higher up in the tree or a new hiding place altogether. But where would that be? If he flew into another tree, they would see him. If he chose the barn, they would follow him. Likewise if he ran behind any of the straw stacks, they would follow there.

Oh where, oh where should he go? While the boy was getting off the woodpile was his only chance for the man would soon re-

Billy Whiskers at Home

turn from chasing the young gobbler and turkey hens. At last he decided to run into the barn as there were numerous dark corners there where he could hide. Once his mind was made up, it did

not take long for him to fly out of the tree and, half flying, half running, he made his way to the barn. He went to the back door as that was out of sight of the man who was chasing the other turkeys round and round the barn, over barrels and under fences and about pigsties, with Billy Whiskers getting in his way just when he reached out to take hold of a fowl and it would escape. The man called Billy every name he could think of, and threw stones at him too, but what cared he when he was doing his friends, the turkeys, a good turn? He could not stand by and hear the pitiful call of the turkeys and not try to do something to save them.

Billy Whiskers at Home

Once the man succeeded in catching a young gobbler, and had him under his arm carrying him away to have his head chopped off, when the turkey called, "Billy, save me quickly or it will be too late! He is carrying me to the block to chop off my head! I have seen all my brothers and sisters go this terrible way. Oh, quick, Billy, quick! Do something or it will be too late!"

Billy baaed back to the poor panic-stricken young turkey, "I will! I will save you!" and all the other fowls in the barnyard and even the pigs in the pens and the cows standing around chewing their cuds called out, "Oh, hurry, Billy, hurry or you will be too late!"

The man was almost to the fatal block but Billy was creeping up still closer and closer to him until he was only six feet away. Then with a little bound Billy gave the man a butt that sent man, turkey and all away over the block, the fellow falling on his face and releasing the turkey as he fell. The moment that turkey found itself free it ran toward the barn and quickly disappeared in the darkness within.

The man was so intensely angry at Billy that he picked up a club and started in pursuit of him. But he might just as well have attempted to catch a whirlwind as Billy when he was on the run. However, he chased him away out into the pasture until Billy took the path to the lake. Then he realized it was useless to follow any further as he would be unable to overtake him before he reached the lake, and he knew if he followed that far Billy would swim it and he could not do that in late November with any comfort. So back he went to the barnyard grumbling to himself, "Well, if I can't catch that turkey, I will another if I have to stay up all night to do it!"

When he reached the barnyard he heard Mr. Watson and Hiram as well as the two boys laughing so he hurried on to see what they were finding so funny. He arrived just as it was all over, though he did see Hiram shaking himself and picking hay out of his hair with one hand as with the other he held out to Mr. Watson the big turkey gobbler, dead. Yes, the one that had been up in the tree and had run to the barn to hide. He had flown into the mow to hide and Hiram had seen a long turkey feather fluttering on the hay of the loft as if it had just been dropped. Climbing up the ladder, he saw Mr. Turkey trying to hide himself in the hay. After a long chase and many a fall for both man and turkey, as hay is difficult to run on, Hiram succeeded in catching him. He was going toward the ladder to descend to the barn floor and in the dim light of the mow he did not see the hay chute. Before he knew it, he had walked straight into the opening and had slid to the bottom, landing on his head and shoulders, but with the turkey still clasped to his breast. In some way the turkey's neck had been twisted in the fall and when they looked at him after

Billy Whiskers at Home

Hiram stood up, they found him dead. But he died in a good cause for the next day he with two other turkeys made all the family and several of their most intimate neighbors happy as they feasted on his tender meat thickly covered with rich gravy.

Such a dinner as that was! The table fairly groaned under the load of goodies. Two tables had been put together and they extended through the dining room into the living room, furnishing seats for twenty, to say nothing of a third table spread for the children so they would not have to wait until the grown-ups had eaten. You see Mrs. Watson thought it cruel to make children wait when in all probability they were hungrier than the grown-ups as children always have healthy appetites while some adults suffer with dyspepsia. There were several servants to wait on the table, as Mrs. Watson had seen to that. She did not like to jump up and down when she acted as hostess. And neither did she have the dinner served in courses, with the exception of the soup and dessert.

The tables were most tastily decorated with strings of cranberries and the dishes were garnished with all sorts of flowers cut from vegetables. There were roses cut from beets, white roses formed from mashed potatoes, tulips cut out of yellow carrots, and so forth. The turkeys were festooned with cranberries and surrounded with vegetable flowers. But the most gorgeous thing on the entire table was a graceful basket of fruit and flowers combined. Here and there peeked out a yellow grapefruit beside a red, red apple, while a bunch of blue or white grapes cuddled next a banana or tangerine, all arranged in a most artistic manner, with a bunch of huge Malaga grapes tied to the handle with a bright scarlet ribbon bow.

This basket was flanked on either side by a little pig roasted whole with a red apple in its mouth, while at both ends of the table rested the big twenty-pound turkeys browned to a turn. Here and there were vegetable dishes heaped high with fluffy mashed potatoes sprinkled with paprika. There were also candied sweet potatoes half hidden in their candy dip, while sparkling glass dishes held molds of cranberries, preserved cherries, pickled peaches, candied watermelon rind and many kinds of salted nuts. All these things were on the tables at once, including a delectable fruit salad. After the table was cleared of these viands, the dessert was carried in, and I know all the guests wondered how they could eat it. It consisted of mince pie, apple pie, cranberry pie and pumpkin pie served with cheese, followed by ice-cream with chocolate sauce poured over it, angel cake, chocolate layer cake and nut cake, while sweet cider made right on the farm sparkled in the glasses and the aroma of the best of coffee arose from the cups.

"I shall not be able to eat for a week after this dinner, Mrs. Watson," said one of her guests on leaving the table.

"Oh, yes, you will," replied the hostess. "Mr. Watson always

Billy Whiskers at Home

says the same thing but by seven-thirty he is ready to eat again and he says, 'Did I hear you say, mama (that is what he always calls me) that we are not going to have any supper after our late dinner? Well, I don't mind much, but I feel as if I could wash down a small piece of cold turkey and a stalk or two of celery.' And I always tell him if he feels that way, to go to the ice-box and help himself. Which he does and I can't see but what he eats as heartily as if he had not had such a heavy dinner. But then he is so passionately fond of turkey and the things which go with it."

After dinner the men were smoking and the ladies were upstairs primping and chatting when every one was startled by the most terrific banging of tin cans. It sounded as if a whole tin shop was being wrecked.

They all ran to the windows to see what was happening and what they saw caused gales of laughter, for there was Billy Whiskers running around frantically trying to get the ice-cream freezer off his head. He had been nosing around and, discovering the freezer, had tasted the salt on the ice. In endeavoring to get more of the salt, Billy had upset the whole thing and his horns had been caught in the tub that held the freezer and the ice pack. The more he tried to get the tub off his head, the more it stuck.

He tossed his head up and down and tried to bang the tub on the ground and smash it, but it was too strongly made to break.

Billy Whiskers at Home

The metal bands held it together. Then he rolled over and over, but no use. He got up and ran as fast as he could, but being unable to see where he was going, the first thing he knew he ran straight into the little duck pond half way down the hill. As he went in, he hit the edge of the tub on the concrete rim of the artificial pond—and he was  free! But Billy was so disgusted that instead of coming out where he leaped in, he swam straight across the pond, climbed out and ran down the hill into the woods where he stayed until he recovered from his chagrin, for no one saw him until noon the next day. Billy could not stand it to have anything or anybody get the better of him.

With the exception of this one slight mishap every person at the dinner and every animal and fowl in the barnyard (for they had a double portion to eat, too, as it was Thanksgiving) declared it was the best Thanksgiving Day they had ever passed.

CHAPTER XIX

BILLY BECOMES A MOVIE ACTOR

BILLY was close beside Mr. Watson's chair, that gentleman sitting under a big elm, his chair tipped back against its trunk, a newspaper in his hands, when a stranger drove into the yard in a high-powered, bright red roadster. He stopped the car and coming up to Mr. Watson, said:

"Have I the pleasure of addressing Mr. Watson?"

"You have," Mr. Watson replied. "What can I do for you?"

"I have come to see if I can buy that fine looking goat beside you."

"I fear you cannot. We are very fond of this goat, and he has been a great pet with us for years. He has been away from us for three years but has just returned. Where he was and with whom I have no way of finding out. All I know is that one day he disappeared and three years after that returned. He is a most surprisingly smart goat."

161

Billy Whiskers at Home

"If you do not know where he has been all that time, I think I know about part of those three years."

"You mean to tell me you think you have seen this goat before—while he was away from my farm?"

"I certainly do, and what is more, I think I can prove it. Have you ever felt deep down in his hair, around his neck?"

"Why, no, I never had any occasion to do that."

"With your permission, I believe I can find something that will prove to you that I have seen this goat before and, in fact, owned him for several months."

"You surprise me! Certainly I give you permission to feel around his neck if you wish to do so."

In less than a minute, the man had run his fingers through Billy's hair and had brought to view a small but strongly linked gold chain

Billy Whiskers at Home

with a round flat disk of gold hanging from it, which bore some engraving.

"Will you kindly read what it says on the disk?" he asked.

Mr. Watson took it and adjusting his glasses on his nose leaned over Billy and read:

This badge was presented
to
BILLY WHISKERS
for his bravery in saving the life of a child
from a burning building
in the
town of Plumbville
on May sixth, in the year 1921

"This is most astonishing news! But I can well believe it. Billy is so smart and so brave. He is absolutely fearless," said Mr. Watson.

"I suppose you would want quite a high price for him if you sold him," responded the man.

"Yes, I should, but I haven't the least idea of selling him. We are all too fond of him for that."

"I am very much disappointed. But could I not induce you to change your mind, if I offered you the largest sum that has ever been given for a goat?"

Billy Whiskers at Home

"No. Money cannot buy Billy Whiskers. I shall keep him until he dies of old age, or I do," said Mr. Watson.

"I am more sorry than I can tell you, as I wanted particularly to have him act in a high-class movie I am putting on the screen. You see when I owned him, or thought I owned him, he was my best drawing card in the movies."

Mr. Watson began to laugh. It struck him as funny that Billy, who had done nearly everything, to be sure, had also been in the movies. "But when I think of it, I don't know why he should *not* be a success in the movies, for he was a first-class actor in the circus for two or three years," he said.

"Mr. Watson, if you could only see the pleasure he gives to little children when he is acting in the movies, I am sure you would let me have him. The films he is in are shown at orphan asylums, reform schools, charity fairs and so on."

"Oh, is that so? Well, I certainly like to give pleasure to poor little orphans. Tell you what I will do. I'll *loan* him to you, but I won't sell him to anyone."

"You are just the big-hearted man I thought you were, Mr. Watson!" exclaimed the caller. "And I thank you for the loan of him. We will take the best of care of him. In fact, he will have a caretaker who does nothing but look after his health and comfort. Why, when I had him before, I had his life insured and a veterinary to look after his health and to oversee his food. He was bathed and his hair combed and perfumed as if he was a human being, while he had a big ten by ten foot box stall all to himself, and rode in a limousine to and from the studio. Oh, I can tell you he was treated like a king, and he will have the same treatment again.

"If you would like to hear, I will tell you the special stunt we want him to do now. Picture to yourself a mountain fastness with two high peaks, between them a deep cleft or cut thousands of feet deep. On one side stands Billy with a young baby strapped to his back, the mother standing beside him wringing her hands in agony as she is about to make him leap across the chasm. She has been kidnaped by bandits and carried into the mountains. They did not know she had a baby under her shawl when they kidnaped her, and when they made the discovery they were going to kill the child, but she thought of this way of saving the baby's life. You see the goat belonged to her next-door neighbor in the village at the foot of the mountain, and the mother was sure the goat would take it home."

"You don't think Billy will take that part, now do you?" asked Mr. Watson.

"I know he will, for I have seen him do much more difficult parts."

Billy Whiskers at Home

"Well, if that is the kind of thing he does, I certainly want to see him act for the movies," said Mr. Watson.

"You certainly shall. When the first film is put on, I will send you a pass book with enough tickets in it to take your family and intimate friends. Now I must be going, or I shall be unable to reach Chicago by nightfall. And if you have no objection, I will take Billy right along with me in the car. There isn't much room in this roadster, but I know he has ridden in roadsters before and enjoys it and so I will have no difficulty keeping him in the car. You may be interested to know we make all our films at the Essenay Studios in Chicago."

Billy had been listening to all the two men had said, but when he heard he was to be taken away from his family then and there, he jumped to his feet and went bounding to the stable yard to tell them. For how awful it would be for him to be carried off and not have a chance to tell them where he was going! He was glad he was not going to be sold, though to be loaned was almost as bad as there was no knowing how long the man would keep him.

"Jehoshaphat!" exclaimed Mr. Watson. "One would think he understood what we were saying, for he lay there as quiet as a mouse until we spoke of taking him away and then he fled."

"I expect he is tired of being away from home as you say he has just returned after nearly a three-year absence. He surely is smart

Billy Whiskers at Home

and I really believe he understands almost everything he hears. I know we all thought so at the studio when he was with us."

"I am afraid we will have a time to catch him," said Mr. Watson. "There he is in the barnyard in the midst of a crowd. I believe he is telling them he is going to be taken away, for see how downhearted Nannie looks, and the way she hangs her head shows she is unhappy. The minute he sees us start for the barnyard he will run away and we will be unable to capture him."

"I have a plan. I will drive away, go to town and have my luncheon, and he will think I have departed for good and all. Then while I am away, you try to shut him in the barn and have him ready for me on my return, which will be right after luncheon."

"I am sorry you have to go, for I was thinking of having the pleasure of your company at my own table and having you tell us what Billy did in the movies."

"I am very sorry I cannot accept your kind invitation, but I have a little business in the town before I go back to Chicago."

After Mr. Swan, the movie man, had gone, Mr. Watson went in the house to tell his wife about Billy and how he had loaned him to Mr. Swan to act in the movies for a little while. "But how to capture the foxy old fellow is more than I know," he concluded.

"You will have a difficult time of it, for he will be suspicious of you for a few days now," replied his wife.

Billy Whiskers at Home

"I have it!" exclaimed Mr. Watson. "I'll pick a bushel of carrots that he loves so dearly, and take them into the barn, where I shall leave them and go on about my business, never so much as looking in his direction. And I shall be greatly surprised and disappointed if when I am out of sight, he does not go straight to the barn to get some. When I know he is in the barn, I will slip around and shut the door, and then I shall have him safe enough."

Everything proceeded splendidly up to closing the barn door. But the minute Billy heard it slam he suspected foul play and without a moment's delay he rushed through the barn to an open door on the opposite side, and through this he went like a shot, running to a little shed that sheltered the mowing machine in winter. It was dark as pitch in there, which he knew would aid him if no one saw him enter. But alas for Billy! Mrs. Watson had been watching her husband's maneuvers from the sitting room window, and quickly came out to tell her husband where Billy was hiding. Then Mr. and Mrs. Watson and their hired man all crept up to the shed and had Billy cornered like a rat in a trap before he was aware of it. Mr. Watson and his hired man soon had a rope around his

168

Billy Whiskers at Home

neck and were leading him out of the shed when Mr. Swan returned. He drove right into the barnyard and Billy was forced to jump into the car where he was securely tied. Then amidst the fluttering of fowls and the distressed baaing of his family, handsome Billy Whiskers was driven off to become a movie actor in Chicago.

THE END

The
Billy Whiskers Series

SAALFIELD

By
Frances
Trego
Montgomery

The antics of frolicsome Billy Whiskers, that adventuresome goat Mrs. Montgomery writes about in these stories make all the boys and girls chuckle—and every story that is issued about him is pronounced by them "better than the last."

TITLES IN SERIES

1. Billy Whiskers
2. Billy Whiskers' Kids
3. Billy Whiskers, Junior
4. Billy Whiskers' Travels
5. Billy Whiskers at the Circus
6. Billy Whiskers at the Fair
7. Billy Whiskers' Friends
8. Billy Whiskers, Jr., and His Chums
9. Billy Whiskers' Grandchildren
10. Billy Whiskers' Vacation
11. Billy Whiskers Kidnaped
12. Billy Whiskers' Twins
13. Billy Whiskers in an Aeroplane
14. Billy Whiskers in Town
15. Billy Whiskers in Panama
17. Billy Whiskers at the Exposition
18. Billy Whiskers Out West
19. Billy Whiskers in the South
20. Billy Whiskers in Camp
21. Billy Whiskers in France
22. Billy Whiskers' Adventures
23. Billy Whiskers in the Movies
24. Billy Whiskers Out for Fun
25. Billy Whiskers' Frolics
26. Billy Whiskers at Home

BOUND IN BOARDS

COVER IN COLORS

PROFUSE TEXT ILLUSTRATIONS

FULL-PAGE DRAWINGS IN COLORS

THE SAALFIELD PUBLISHING COMPANY—AKRON, OHIO

The Billy Whiskers Game

No. 280

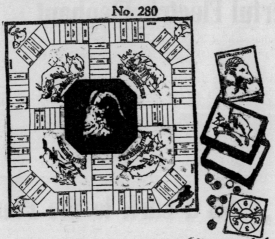

A million delighted youngsters have read the

BILLY WHISKERS BOOKS

THERE'S A LAUGH ON EVERY PAGE

The same delighted youngsters (and their parents too) will play the new board game where Billy DOES all the things the stories tell.

THERE'S A LAUGH AT EVERY PLAY

The Billy Whiskers Game

"The Game's The Thing!"